Ministering Spirits Series Book One

UNSEEN

Author
Virginia Murphy's
Daughter-in-law
Jill Murphy

Ministering Spirits Series Book One

UNSEEN

J.R. MESSENGER

Pleasant Word

© 2005 by J.R. Messenger. All rights reserved.

Pleasant Word (a division of WinePress Publishing, PO Box 428, Enumclaw, WA 98022) functions only as book publisher. As such, the ultimate design, content, editorial accuracy, and views expressed or implied in this work are those of the author.

No part of this publication may be reproduced, stored in a retrieval system or transmitted in any way by any means—electronic, mechanical, photocopy, recording or otherwise—without the prior permission of the copyright holder, except as provided by USA copyright law.

Unless otherwise noted, all Scriptures are taken from the Holy Bible, New International Version, Copyright © 1973, 1978, 1984 by the International Bible Society. Used by permission of Zondervan Publishing House. The "NIV" and "New International Version" trademarks are registered in the United States Patent and Trademark Office by International Bible Society.

Scripture references marked KJV are taken from the King James Version of the Bible.

Scripture references marked NASB are taken from the New American Standard Bible, © 1960, 1963, 1968, 1971, 1972, 1973, 1975, 1977 by The Lockman Foundation. Used by permission.

ISBN 1-4141-0492-8
Library of Congress Catalog Card Number: 2005904411

Dedication

To my wonderful husband Tom,
Thanks for all your support,
patience and encouragement.

And to great friend's and proofreader's
Gayle Dye and Connie Patten.
It's a blessing to know you
And the joyful spirit within you.

So we fix our eyes not on what is seen, but on what is unseen. For what is seen is temporary, but what is unseen is eternal.
—*2 Cor. 4:18* (NIV)

Prologue

Darwin slumped over on his barstool stirring his drink with the straw. The dark spirit to his right made the same stirring motion in Darwin's head with a claw like finger. While the unseen dark spirit on Darwin's left whispered taunting thoughts in his ear. *'Go ahead, drink another one, it'll make you feel better. After a few more you'll forget all about your wife leaving you. All she ever did was nag you about drinking anyway. You don't need her. Whiskey is the only friend you've got. It's the only thing that's always been there for you, so go ahead have another.'*

Darwin glanced at the clock on the wall, just after eleven; the night was still young. "Bartender...gi'me another." Darwin shouted over a whiskey thick tongue.

"Sorry, I think you've had enough, I'm gonna have to cut you off." The bartender offered his apology.

Darwin guzzled the last of his drink and slammed down the empty glass. "Come on Joe, just one more then I'll go."

"One more and I'll have to call you a stretcher instead of a cab."

Darwin bellowed out a few obscenities that the dark spirit whispered into his ear as he left the bar.

At his car he fumbled and dropped his keys three times before getting the driver's door unlocked. His head spun like rotating liquid as he tried to find the ignition. One of the dark spirits still stirring up his thoughts with one finger, while the other whispered terrible notions into his head. His legs were so rubbery and uncontrollable that he revved the motor to the red line when he finally started the car. His heavy foot made jerky stops every time he changed gears, from reverse, to forward, to his stop before exiting the parking lot. Once he was on the road his foot grew heavier, as one of the dark spirits pressed it against the accelerator.

'Faster, go faster. Find your wife. Tell her you don't need her. There are plenty of other women out there. You're not that worthless. You can find another woman.' The dark spirit continued to whisper tor-

Prologue

menting thoughts in Darwin's head. *'Hurry up... faster...faster. Crash into a light pole. Just end it all. That's the easiest way to solve all your problems. That's the only way to end your misery.'*

Darwin's foot grew heavier as his resistance weakened. Tires squalled as he turned the corner without slowing down. Thoughts pounding through his throbbing head as he sped down the dark street.

Suddenly a car appeared in the intersection, out of no where. Darwin didn't even have time to break before making impact with the driver's side door. He totally missed the stop sign, or was it a traffic light? All he knew was that both cars were now skidding out of control straight for a light pole. He caught a glimpse of the young girl's terrified face just before impact with the pole, and then everything went black.

An hour later on a ranch south of Dodge City a loud noise bolted Rachel up out of bed. "Was that a gunshot or one of the mares kicking through a stall?" She whispered to herself as she looked at the clock and then out the window. A light from the barn office blazed out into the darkness.

Rachel went to Lisa's room to find out why she'd left the light on. After knocking with no response, she opened the door and saw that Lisa's bed was still made. Which meant Lisa was still in the barn writing the letter she claimed couldn't wait until morning.

It was a warm July night, yet Rachel shivered as she walked out the front door right through the unseen entity on her porch. Rubbing her bare arms, to ward off the chill, she continued on to the barn.

When Rachel opened the office door her breath caught sharply in her throat. Lisa was lying on the floor surrounded by a crimson pool. With a trembling hand she found Lisa's weak pulse. Quickly she turned to the desk on her right for the phone. Before she could pick up the receiver she heard a gunshot outside. Without hesitation she switched direction and opened a small wooden box on the desktop that contained rifle shells. Grabbing a couple shells, then reaching for the rifle over the door, she loaded the rifle as she made her way out. Her hurried steps were in rhythm with her racing pulse.

She raced blindly through the darkness until a bright flash from another gunshot showed her the way. The killer was near the brood mare pen. Her strides grew faster as her adrenaline quickened. *'What am I going to do when I'm face to face with this killer?'* her mind raced. If she could see the angel rushing ahead of her, she'd have no fear. But all she

Prologue

saw was the man's face as he turned to see who was running up behind him. Stopping dead in her tracks she nearly dropped the rifle once she realized who it was. '*No,*' her mind screamed, too stunned to breathe the word out loud.

Chapter 1

Evelyn woke from a deep sleep to the sound of rumbling thunder and her mother's urgent calls.

"Eve…Eve can you hear me?" Peggy called out over a dry throat. "I need some water."

"I'm coming mother." Evelyn called back. Knowing her mother was waiting for the assurance that she was awake. "Lord I'm going to need your help to continue caring for my mother. Between my blindness and her worsening arthritis we're not a very compatible duo." Eve prayed under her breath as she felt her way to the kitchen.

Flashes of lightening pierced through the darkness like strobe lights. Followed immediately by rumbles of thunder. Eve knew that meant the storm was directly overhead. The rain pounding against the rooftop was as furious as the earth-shaking rumbles.

With one hand she held the glass, her other hand reached for the faucet. A flash of lightening lit up the darkness. It was bright enough to cause even her blind eyes to close against its brilliance. At that same instant a powerful jolt ran through Eve. A force that slammed her to the floor. The deafening clap of thunder shattered the window over the sink along with the glass in her hand.

"What happened? Did you drop the glass?" Peggy called out again when there was no response. "Eve...what happened?"

Peggy reached for her cane and struggled to her feet, still calling out to her daughter, but rumbles of thunder were the only reply she heard. She slowly made her way downstairs to the kitchen. She shivered with fear when she found Eve spread out on the tile floor. Fragments of shattered glass were everywhere. Eve's hand was bleeding from the broken glass she still clutched. "Please Lord, let the breath of life still be in her. Please!" Her hazel eyes filled with concern. She tightened her grip on the cane until her knuckles whitened. Then she slowly bent down and felt Eve's neck for a pulse. "Thank you, Lord." She sighed with relief. It was irregular, but it was a pulse.

Peggy's hand trembled as she reached for the wall phone. After calling 911, she dialed her son, Keith, who lived just two blocks north of them. He could be there long before the EMS unit arrived.

Without moving Eve's body, Keith made sure she was breathing on her own. He cleared away the glass and got the bleeding stopped. Then he comforted his mother until the EMS arrived. Keith was a physical therapist, not a physician like his father, yet Peggy didn't seem to see any difference.

At Dodge City's hospital Peggy watched Keith pace the emergency room floor. Worry was written all over his face, as it was on hers. They've heard that lightening strike victims don't always survive. "I shouldn't have asked her for that water." She combed trembling fingers through her short gray hair.

"Mom, stop beating yourself up. How could you've known?" Keith stopped pacing long enough to look his mother in the eye. The hazel color was dulled with deep concern. Dark rings were already forming under her eyes from the missed sleep. "If it'll make you feel better I'll call your minister and get the church to start praying for her right now."

Peggy glanced at the clock on the wall. Three A.M. "No, that can wait a few more hours. I hate to make anyone else lose sleep. Besides, I've been praying for her under my breath ever since I found her."

Keith shrugged his wide shoulders and resumed his pacing, saying his own little prayer as he paced. It had been years since he attended church – four years to be exact, but he still believed there was a God up there listening. He just hadn't kept the dedication that Eve and Peggy had. Every Sunday they were there. Seeing Eye dog, canes and all. Keith had stopped going after their father's death.

Their father, Charles, had kept his heart condition secret, so they were all stunned by his sudden heart attack. Especially since Charles was a heart surgeon. He was also the biggest procrastinator when it came to taking care of himself. His first thoughts and concerns were always of others.

Eve had been the only one who found optimism in their father's death. But Eve was always the optimist in the family. Even in her own blindness she had always seen hope in every situation. It was obvious to her family that she found strength in the joy the Lord had given her. And he had given her an abundant amount of joy in her thirty years.

"Mrs. Kincaid."

Peggy's eyes darted towards the doorway at the familiar voice calling her name. She instantly recognized the gray-haired doctor looking back at her.

Dr. Howard J. Bowman, he'd been close friends with Charles. "Yes, Howard."

"Your daughter is stabilized, but...I'm afraid... she's in a coma." His eyes clouded over with regret at being the bearer of bad news. Especially at the sight of Peggy's hand covering her mouth to muffle the cry in her throat. He instantly went to her side. Sitting down next to her, he draped a comforting arm around her shoulders.

Peggy buried her face into his shoulder and let her tears spill over his blue scrubs. "How long do you think it will last?"

"Honestly," With a heavy sigh he forced out a reply. "we can never be sure how long a person will stay comatose. I'm so sorry I had to be the one to tell you this."

His response caused her to cry harder.

"Better to come from someone we know." Keith tried to ease the doctor's guilt. Then he pried Peggy off the doctor's sleeve. "Come on mom, I'll take you home. There's nothing we can do here. Besides, I've got to get back and board up that broken window."

"I'm not going anywhere except to see Eve. I want to sit with her." Peggy tried to nudge Keith away, but he was too strong.

"Mom, you know there's nothing you can do and no reason you need to stay here tonight. Let me take you home to get some rest, then I'll bring you back later, okay?" Keith's soft blue eyes studied her weary face.

"He's right Peggy." Bowman agreed helping Peggy to her feet. "You should go and get some rest. I'll be here 'til eight A.M. and I can call you if there's any change."

"You promise you'll call right away if there's the slightest change, and you'll tell the next doctor to do the same? I need to be here when she wakes up." She spoke through her sobs.

Bowman's nod was confirmation enough. Peggy stopped resisting Keith and let him lead her out of the hospital. Once in the car she even agreed to go to Keith's house and rest there. She knew she could get back to the hospital quicker that way, since Keith was a few blocks closer. Plus Peggy hadn't driven since she went off her arthritis medication, which had been nearly a year now.

For over a month Peggy sat with Eve all day, everyday, from sunup to sunset. She prayed for a miraculous healing upon Eve. By the thirtieth day she began to doubt that God was even listening to her prayers. That's when she began fasting one meal a day hoping to either gain God's attention or hear a reply. By day forty she had dropped ten pounds, but not one ounce of hope.

Sitting around the hospital gave Peggy plenty of time to read and reflect over her children's lives. She couldn't help but feel Eve had been shortchanged. Dealing with the functional blindness since birth and losing her father at twenty-six, only to be left caring for a grief stricken mother. Eve had never even had the chance to marry, let alone time to fall in love. Now this…a coma. Peggy was having a hard time understanding God's plan or purpose. That's why she continually prayed for a miracle to bring Eve back to her.

Eve had been an exceptional student at Sacred Heart Academy, excelling in everything she laid her hands on, from reading Braille, to speaking Spanish. Then eight years ago Eve's Aunt Maggy mentioned Eve becoming a court reporter. The idea was an instant spark of hope in Eve's career darkened future. Within a year Eve had mastered her stenography skills and got a part time job at the courthouse. Within another year they had moved her into a full time court reporter position.

Neither one of Eve's brother's had any health or vision problems, not even as much as needing glasses. They hadn't even had any other major problems to overcome other than losing their father. Keith was a physical therapist, and Troy was a heart surgeon like their father. They were both married, but Keith was the only one with a child so far. Troy lived in Wichita and claimed they were both too busy to start a family, since his wife was a RN at the hospital where he worked.

Because of Eve's condition, Troy finally made a visit to Dodge City for the first time in four years, since the funeral. Even the holidays hadn't been enough to persuade him to visit. And it was only a three-hour drive between Wichita and Dodge City. Yet two days was all Peggy could talk Troy into staying.

Peggy's trance was broken when Keith walked into Eve's hospital room. Because Charles had been a surgeon at the hospital, they had managed to get Eve a private room, instead of putting her with the other comatose patients.

Peggy knew Keith was there to drive her home. Cupping Eve's hand between hers, she pulled it to her lips, and placed a gentle kiss on the back of her hand. "I'll see you tomorrow, Sleeping Beauty." A single tear fell onto Eve's hand, and it flinched ever so slightly, but it was enough that Peggy noticed it. "Ooh! Keith, her hand twitched. That's the first sign of movement since…" Elation gleamed from her hazel eyes and rang out in her voice.

"Twitches happen mom, so don't let yourself get all worked up over nothing." Keith was just trying to be logical.

Peggy scolded him with a look. "It wasn't nothing. It was something! And I'm not going to let you steal my joy."

Keith's hands flew up in defense. "Okay. Can we go now? Lou Ann's warming up dinner for you." He reached for her arm, but she pulled it from his reach.

"Thank you, but I'm still fasting." She moved towards the door with more hesitation than usual.

"You've got to start eating better mom." Keith inhaled deeply as he followed her out the door. "Lou Ann made roast beef, your favorite."

"Don't you tempt me young man."

Keith ran a frustrated hand through his dark hair. He followed her the rest of the way out in silence. He knew there was little that could change her mind once it was set on something. Which is where Eve must have gotten her determination.

Chapter 2

It was seven minutes after midnight when Eve bolted upright in bed. She blinked as her eyes began adjusting to the dim lighting. Her heartbeat quickened with excitement as things started coming into focus.

"What…I can see! I must have died and gone to heaven!" Eve's eyes widened to the size of Granny Smith apples matching her shade of green. She couldn't believe her eyes. They were working! Her eyes were working. "I never imagined heaven would be this dark. So where am I? I must be dreaming, but even in my wildest dreams I've never seen things like this. In all these glorious colors."

"You are in the hospital." A vaguely familiar voice came from her left.

Eve's head quickly turned to see who was in the room with her. The sight she beheld was indescribable to her own mind, since she had never seen before, but what her eyes took in was a pure delight to her heart and soul.

A large muscular man in a radiant white suit sat on a chair to the left of her bed. His hair gleamed like golden strands of silk. Even his skin emitted a soft luminous glow. His eyes were as blue as a cloudless sky. Yet the pupils of his eyes blazed like dual infernos. It might have been enough to frighten the average person, but for Eve it was pure splendor for her eyes to behold such a sight.

Eve glanced around the rest of the small room. The window behind the man revealed only darkness outside. Next to the window was a door to a dimly lit bathroom. Then to her right there was a door to a hallway along with another chair.

"You sound vaguely familiar, but I'm afraid I might not recognize you by sight if you were my own brother. So who are you?" Eve finally turned her attention back to the man.

"I am Hamuel, your watcher."

"Hamuel...my *watcher*! I don't understand. I've never heard that name before. Are you on watch for the hospital or something?" Eve shook her auburn head in confusion.

Laughter rolled from his throat. It was a sweet joyful sound that curled her lips instantly into a smile. The laughter sounded as if it were reverberating through water. It was like nothing she'd ever heard before.

"Forgive me for laughing. I am just not used to this yet. I have been speaking to you all your life. Although your physical ears have only been able to hear me for the past forty days, but you were unable to respond. That is why my voice would sound familiar to you. We have been called ministering spirits, watchmen, watchers, guardians, or angels, whichever you prefer."

Eve's mind raced to take in everything he'd just said. But she still couldn't imagine being able to see or talk to angels. So she had to be in heaven. And from what he was saying she must have been there for forty days. So was she in some type of waiting chamber? Is that why it was so dimly lit? Was she awaiting her judgement? Was Hamuel there to take her to the throne room? Why didn't he have wings if he was an angel?

"There's hospitals in heaven?" Eve shot him a dumbfounded look. "And if you're an angel, where's your wings?"

Hamuel broke into that sweet sound of laughter once more. "No, my dear girl. You have not died. You have been in a coma the past forty days. Now you have been given the gift of sight. Physical *and* spiritual. You can see into both realms." He shrugged his shoulders before answering the later question. "As for my wings, they remain hidden until they are in need."

"And when is that?"

"When it is time to battle the dark forces. Which you will see soon enough, so do not be alarmed when you do. I have successfully protecting you for thirty years. I must also tell you now, I will not answer all your questions. Some things must remain a mystery in this life and some things I myself do not even know." His head would have touched the ceiling if he hadn't stooped over when he stood up. He walked around the chair to look out the window. It clarified his phenomenal size when he crossed his powerful arms over his wide chest.

Eve looked down over her small-blanketed frame to compare her size to his. Which was no comparison at all. Hamuel had to be around eight or nine feet tall and well over 300 pounds of solid muscle. He was more than two of her. She knew she was only 5'5" and a mere 120 pounds at her last doctor's visit.

Eve questioned why her mother had never mentioned him to her before. Then Hamuel explained that she was the only one who'd be able to see him or anything else in the spiritual realm. Which brought her to the next question of why she was the only one allowed to see into the spiritual realm. He said that anyone else would be too terrified to see some of the things that she would see. He also told her it was all part of her mission. But he couldn't tell her what that mission was, since he didn't even know that yet.

When she asked about his name and if he had a last name, he told her that it meant "warmth of God", and how angels only had one name. She was about to ask another question, but he raised a finger to his mouth to hush her. His gaze was fixed intently on something out the window.

"What is it?" She whispered.

"There are two on the roof discussing something. I need to hear what they are saying."

Eve's brow creased with confusion. She had to see what *two* he was talking about. She pulled off the IV, electrodes and all the other restraints holding her down. Tossing back the covers she got up.

When the heart monitor alarm sounded Hamuel waved a hand to silence it.

Her knees buckled when she applied weight to them. They were weak from the lack of use.

She caught and steadied herself on the bed, then continued on toward the window.

Her eyes followed Hamuel's gaze. At first all she could see was darkness until they moved. They were on a lower rooftop that extended out from the emergency room entrance. They looked like 3-D shadows or charcoal gray statues with wings. The sight of them made Eve cringe. Their eyes were like two solid black marbles, void of emotion or life.

When one of them looked in their direction. Hamuel reached out for Eve's arm and pushed her behind him in a protective manner. In a fright filled breath she thought she smelled a bouquet of wild flowers, but there were none in her room, so with another deep breath she determined the sweet fragrance was coming from Hamuel. Which was something else she found familiar.

Without asking she knew they were part of the dark forces Hamuel had mentioned.

When his arm lowered he turned to her. "They have gone."

"You mean you could actually hear what they were saying?"

He nodded in response. "They were discussing the poor tortured soul they have been enticing with alcohol. He was brought into emergency tonight. The dark ones were angry because they were not successful. They wanted his spirit, but the breath of life would not leave his body. Someone is lifting up strong prayers for this man. That was the only grace that saved him." He turned back to the window again. "They said the crash should have ended his life as it did the girl."

Eve put her hands to her head and massaged her temples. Her head was beginning to ache from all the overwhelming information, and all the adjustments her eyes were not used to making.

Her touch suddenly made her want to see what she looked like. She had a vague idea from her touch sensory, but she wanted a clear picture of herself. She rushed into the bathroom hoping to find a mirror. Flicking on the light she found what she was looking for. Once her eyes adjusted to the brighter light she saw...her unfamiliar face.

A wave of cinnamon colored hair laid in a tangled mess down over her shoulders. Her nose and cheeks were small and round just as she had imagined. Her skin tone was pale, with full lips and teeth as white as the hospital walls.

With an index finger she touched the small mole below her left eye. For years she had wondered what that small bump looked like. She never realized it was so dark. Her eyes were green like Granny Smith apples, just as her mother had told her they were, only now she knew exactly what that color was. Her eyelashes were thick, and as dark as the mole, so it gave the appearance of a fine line around her eyes.

Her hand touched the cold smooth image in the mirror. Looking closer she saw a flicker of light inside her pupils. At that moment Hamuel appeared in the doorway. She quickly looked to him in question.

"You are a child of light. Your eyes are the lamp of your body. Therefore they reflect the light of Christ within you." Hamuel knew her question before she asked.

"You must truly be an angel if you can read my mind."

Hamuel let out another soft pleasant laugh. "No. I can not read your mind. The question was merely written on your face. The Spirit of God is the only Spirit that searches your heart and can read what is inside you."

"So, if I see someone that doesn't have a flickering light in their eyes, does that mean…" She swallowed hard, nearly choking on the thought. "…they're children of darkness?"

He nodded in response. "Read Luke eleven verses thirty four through thirty six. It will help you better understand. It is also in Matthew six."

"I do recall reading something like that. I just never imagined it would be a literal light showing in our eyes."

"Only because you can see these things. Others do not see the light or the darkness in man as you can."

Eve turned back to the mirror. Her eyes misted over with tears. A rush of emotion flooded over her. "Why has God blessed me with so much? Or is this a curse? What can I possibly do with this knowledge? Why has he given it to someone so unworthy?"

"The Creator has chosen you for his purpose. So do not say you are unworthy." His voice was stern as he looked down at her. "To say that would mean that God sent his Son to suffer without reason. This *is* a blessing and he *will* reveal the purpose when the time is right."

Eve rushed past Hamuel so fast she wasn't sure if she went around him or through him. Yet the hair-raising thought only caused her to pause for an instant. "I've got to find a nurse and get an aspirin." She rubbed her temples as she continued out of the room.

Chapter 3

Eve went to the elevators, since the nurse's station was abandoned. She rubbed her temples again in desperate need of a pain reliever. She pushed a button to the elevator hoping to find a nurse on another floor. When Eve got off the elevator she paused to listen. She still had very acute hearing so her ears guided her towards the noise.

She was nearly run over by a gurney when she reached the emergency room hall. She shuddered at the sight of the girl's bloody torso as it was rushed past. She'd obviously been shot in the stomach.

What Eve saw next sent a shiver through her. Two dark hissing spirits rushed by chasing after the girl's gurney. The largest one reached the gurney just before it disappeared through a set of swinging doors. He lashed out and pulled the girls spirit right out of her body.

Eve grabbed her chest and inhaled sharply. The smell of sulfur burned her nostrils and caused her to choke on her breath.

Her reaction caused the dark spirits to turn and look at her. His black lifeless eyes narrowed to study her intently. His gray gargoyle like face curled into a snarl to reveal his sharp teeth. When her eyes widened in fear, it made it clear that she saw him. Still holding the girl's limp spirit in his talon grip, he hissed and stepped towards Eve.

Eve turned to run back down the hall as quick as her socks would take her. Hamuel suddenly appeared in front of her, but she couldn't stop in time. So before she realized it, she had run right through him. It was a chilling experience that raised the hairs on her neck once more.

She turned back to see what was happening. Both dark spirits were fleeing from Hamuel with the girl's spirit in tow. Over her thundering heartbeat Eve could barely hear the girls' fading cries for help. She didn't understand why Hamuel wasn't pursuing them to rescue the girl. "Can't you help her?" Eve questioned in breathless compassion.

Hamuel turned to her with his head hung low. "I am afraid not. I am not her watchman. No one prays for her protection. She did not have the light of God within her. Therefore, she was theirs to take." His intense gaze moved over her face. "Yet *you* should not fear them. Christ Jesus gave you power and authority over all unclean spirits, just as He did His apostles."

Eve grabbed both sides of her head in pain. "I feel like I've woke up in the middle of someone else's nightmare. I need an aspirin."

"Ma'am you need to return to your room." A nurse put an arm around her shoulder and looked at Eve's ID band with her free hand. "Well, you're not even suppose to be in ER. How'd you get way down here, Miss...Evelyn Kincaid? Are you a sleep walker?" The nurse belted out a jolly giggle and ushered Eve to a chair. She called for a nurse from Eve's floor to come get her. While waiting Eve finally got that aspirin she'd been desperately looking for.

Peggy woke in a cold sweat. Her heart running away with her breath. Eve was lying on the kitchen floor burnt to a smoldering crisp with her eyes opened and blazing like fire. She's had the same hideous dream every night since the accident. A dream she keeps praying will go away.

The difference this time was an urgent desire to get to the hospital. A strange sense that Eve needed her. An uneasiness told her something was wrong. It was a feeling that propelled her out of bed. A glance at the clock told her it was three A.M. So she'd have to wait a few more hours since Keith didn't get up until five.

She reached for the water glass on her nightstand, which was another habit that she'd formed since the accident. She took one of her arthritis pills. Which was one good outcome from Eve's accident Peggy was taking her medication regularly again. She was still staying at Keith's, so they helped make sure she took her medicine. Plus Eve needed her again, so she had to be stronger for her daughter's sake.

Peggy picked up her Bible and cane. Then made her way to the rocker in the corner of her room. Reading always helped her get back to sleep after the dreams. She used to never read anything but the King James Version, but for her last birthday Keith had given her a New King James Version, so she had been using it. Since her old Bible had literally fallen apart at the seams.

Daniel was an interpreter of dreams so Peggy had been reading in that book for the past few nights. After reading chapter four she rested her chin in her hand to reflect on what she'd just read. Daniel had a different way of describing angels than most. He referred to them as a watcher, a watchman or a holy one. "God I wish you'd send me a watcher to help me interpret my dream. Why do I keep having this same dream over and over again? Are you trying to prepare me for the loss of my daughter? Oh I pray that's not the case Lord."

The phone rang as if in answer to her question. It startled her so much that she dropped her Bible to the floor when she flinched. It rang out once more before she heard Keith answer it in the next room.

Peggy's heart and head sank low, she feared the call would bear bad news, but she quickly perked up when she heard Keith speak again.

"Wow! That's great. Thanks." Keith hung up the phone and pulled his robe on to tell his mother the good news. Peggy was in the hall waiting on him when he opened his door. "Eve's come out of the coma, but she's a little disoriented. They found her wandering around in the emergency room shocked and confused."

"Praise the Lord. I sensed something was different when I woke up." Peggy cried out as she covered her mouth to stop it from trembling. Tears of joy poured down her face. "It's the miracle I've been praying for. Can we…"

"Get dressed." Keith answered before she finished. He knew what she was going to ask and he'd already planned on going to the hospital anyway.

Peggy walked over to Keith and hugged him out of joy.

"I'm coming too." Lou Ann called out from their bedroom behind Keith.

"Me too." Lexi's ash blond head peered out from her doorway across the hall. With a little balled up hand she rubbed a tired eye.

Keith and Peggy both laughed at the united response.

"Then I guess it's unanimous." Keith added before going back into his room to get dressed.

Eve wasn't in her room when they arrived. The nurse informed them that Dr. Bowman was having a MRI and a CT scan run on Eve. She didn't tell them the good news about Eve being able to see, since Eve had asked to be able to tell them herself. So the nurse simply sent them in her room to wait.

It was nearly two hours later before Eve was brought back to her room. Eve could hardly contain the smile that was aching to burst forth. Seeing everyone in her room and acting like she didn't see a thing took a lot of control. She waited for her mother to speak as the nurse pushed her wheelchair next to the bed. Against her will, the nurse had insisted on making Eve ride in a wheelchair.

"Eve," Peggy spoke softly, as not to startle, once the nurse had left. "I'm here with Keith and his family. We're all so very glad to have you back with us."

"I'd say. It looks like you were all in such a hurry to get here that you didn't give Keith time to brush his hair." Eve's mouth curled into the smile that was no longer confinable.

"What'd you say?" Keith's chin dropped in a dumbfounded look.

"Wouldn't they let you brush your hair?" Eve laughed at the shock on everyone's face. "Yes, I can see it and now I know what the color of black coffee looks like." Eve's mother had referred colors to her through smells that she could relate to. "And salt and pepper." She pointed as she looked at Peggy's short gray boyish haircut. "And honey." She pointed again as she looked at Lou Ann and Lexi.

Keith grinned and smoothed down his hair as he rushed over to her wheel chair. He pulled her up and looked into her eyes. He held up two fingers and a thumb in front of her face. "How many fingers do you see?"

"Two fingers and the big knobby thumb you used to suck on." She wiggled his thumb to insure them she could see it.

Keith grabbed her in a bear hug embrace. "That's the best insult I've ever heard from you."

Eve laughed again as she hugged him back. Then as he pulled away and she saw deep into his eyes she stopped laughing. Before she could say what was on her mind, Lou Ann, Lexi and her mother were all waiting to hug her too. As each one hugged her she looked for the light in their eyes. Her heart began to sink. The only one who had the flicker of light in their eyes was her mother. Eve knew what that meant, but she didn't know what to do with the information at the moment.

They were all curious about how she had gained her eyesight, so she filled them in on what the doctor told her. It wasn't much, since he still didn't know much. All he could figure was that the lightning had somehow corrected the functional blindness, perhaps by stimulating the nerve endings. Which therefore made the nerves function properly. That was the reason for all the tests they wanted to run on her.

"They think I'm either delusional, or that there might be some damage to my optical nerve, since I told them I could see my angel. But I've just been doubly gifted." Eve smiled, but from their stares, she could tell they didn't believe her either. "I'm serious. I can see my angel. Right now he's standing on the ledge just outside my window. His name is Hamuel. I also saw two dark spirits take this girl's soul right out of her body down in ER."

Keith broke out laughing.

Peggy was scowling at them both. She didn't like some of the practical jokes Eve and Keith played on each other. But to joke about spiritual matters was a mockery. "Now Eve, you know how I feel about jokes, but to joke about something like this..."

"Mom, I'm not joking." Eve insisted with all seriousness. She walked over to the window and put her hand to the glass. She couldn't imagine her own family not believing her, especially her mother. "I wish you could see him. I wish I could describe him to you, but I've got to learn my colors by sight before I can really explain him."

"I believe you Auntie." Lexi rushed over and took Eve by the hand. Smiling up at her through trusting denim blue eyes.

Eve smiled back and bent down to hug the six-year-old. "That's why you'll always be my favorite niece."

Eve couldn't convince anyone else that she was actually able to see into the spirit world. In fact, her mother even made her stop talking about it, since she thought she was trying to pull some sort of prank on Keith. It was a deflating feeling in her heart that they wouldn't accept what she was telling them. She never figured they'd think she was delusional too.

When they left to go eat, Eve questioned Hamuel about their disbelief. He simply reminded her how Jesus found few believers in his hometown and how many were his own family. That was one reason why Jesus told his disciples that they must become like a child to enter the kingdom of heaven. Children

Unseen

could believe and trust completely when adults could not, or would not.

Chapter 4

Attorney Adam Webber studied the petite young girl in the orange jumpsuit through the window before entering the room. What was a twenty-five-year-old girl doing in jail on murder charges? A tough break for anyone. She appeared to be praying or crying, he wasn't sure which. With her elbows on the table and her head resting in her hands, her long blond hair concealed her face, yet there was something familiar about her.

He took a deep breath to prepare himself, and then he smoothed down his sandy brown hair with his free hand before reaching for the knob. He'd only defended a total of six murder cases in the whole fourteen years of his career, and that was when he was practicing in Wichita. He never imagined he'd be defending a murder case in Dodge City. Growing up in Dodge, he couldn't even recall hearing about any murders taking place, it was a quiet town for the most part. But then he had to admit, the times were changing quickly around him, everywhere.

The instant Adam opened the door, she looked up, and then it hit him where he'd seen this girl before. She worked at Southwind Quarter Horse Farms, which was the ranch directly south of *his parent's* ranch, on the 640 acres that used to belong to *his family*. Now he knew where those sirens had gone that morning just after one A.M. A knot formed in the pit of his stomach. A murder that close to his parents, that close to him, even closer than merely his own hometown.

"Thank you for coming on such short notice, and on the fourth of July of all days." She stood to offer a hand. "I was hoping it would help, me being your neighbor and all, that is."

"No problem, I'm used to early morning calls in my line of work." He took a seat across the table from her. He propped open his briefcase and took out a notebook and pen. "I haven't yet read the police report, so could you tell me what happened Ms. Meade."

"Please, call me Rachel." She sat back down once he nodded to confirm. "I got up around twelve

thirty, because I thought I heard something. Anyway, I noticed the light still on in the barn office. So then I knocked on my roommates' door, since she was the last one in there. I thought she just forgot to turn off the light or something. When she didn't answer I opened her door. She wasn't there and it didn't look like she'd been there, since her bed was still made. I know she's a neat freak, but she wouldn't make it just to get up to use the bathroom." She pushed her hair behind her ears and took a deep breath before going on. "I figured she was still in the barn writing her letter, although I couldn't imagine why, so I went to check on her."

Rachel blinked back the tears that clouded over her eyes. Once she regained control, she went on. "I never imagined I'd find Lisa lying in a pool of blood on the floor of the office, but I did." Her head fell back into her hands as she cried out. "Who could do this? How could they think I did it? We may have had our differences, but I've never thought about hurting her."

"So tell me, why *do* they think you did this? What do they have on you? And to whom was she writing a letter that couldn't wait until morning?" Adam could tell the girl was truly remorseful, but he needed to hear her plea of innocence. He sat back in his chair to study her face as she spoke. Clicking his pen in and out, he waited for her answer, but his eye's remained fixed on hers.

"I'm not sure who the letter was to. She didn't say and I didn't ask." Rachel sniffled and reached for a tissue. "Anyway, I bent down and felt her weak pulse, then I heard a gun shot outside. I didn't even take a moment to think. I simply grabbed the rifle from the office wall, stuffed a couple bullets in it and ran out the door. I thought the killer was still out there. Then I heard another shot over by the mare's pen. I found out it was Paco running off some coyotes. I never even fired the rifle, but they said it had been fired that night. They took both rifles and put us both in jail until they could determine which weapon had killed Lisa." Rachel shook her head in disbelief. "She was still alive when I raced out of the office."

"Did you see the coyotes?" He went on after she shook her head. "You said the rifle was on the office wall?" He knew the biggest mistake most people made was touching the murder weapon. Things looked even grimmer now than when he first walked through the door. Her prints were obviously all over the weapon, then to top that off she leaves the scene with the gun, and runs smack dab into an eyewitness.

Rachel nodded. Tears welling up once again in her already swollen blue eyes. From the looks of her eyes it was obvious that she had done more crying than sleeping. "Where it always hangs, right over the door, like some kind of trophy or something."

"So who ever used the rifle returned it to its place. Let's just hope he left a fingerprint or two on it." He scribbled something in his notebook. "Where are the bullets kept? Did you notice anything in the office that was out of place? Like a shell casing. Signs of a struggle. Anything?"

"The bullets are kept in a wooden box on top of the desk. I didn't notice anything else." Rachel shook her head. "You said *he*, do you think Paco could have done it? He's such a sweet man. I'd be more apt to think it was Bret. He was constantly making unwanted passes at Lisa and I, and he's so quick-tempered. Especially when getting our rejections all the time. So what do you think my chances are?"

"I think we're going to find out who did this, and I don't think it was you."

"Oh thank you Lord for sending me someone who believes me. I guarantee it wasn't me, Mr. Webber." She shook his hand once more. "Thank you again, so much."

"It will take a few weeks to get all the evidence back from forensics, since it has to be sent off to a lab in Great Bend. But I'll see if we can get you out on bail. Otherwise you'll have to sit in here until this goes before the court."

Chapter 5

Peggy didn't say a word until they all sat down with their breakfast. "Eve must have hit her head hard when she fell." Peggy determined, neatly placing a napkin across her lap. "I just can't imagine any other reason she'd be seeing things like she's saying. I guess we should talk with the doctor before going back to her room."

"Didn't the nurse say that Dr. Booker wouldn't even be here until eight to evaluate her eyes?" Lou Ann stirred her coffee. Then looked up at Peggy, the question glittering in her sapphire eyes. She already knew the answer, but out of habit she used one of her teacher strategies, to jog Peggy's memory.

Peggy nodded. She didn't like Lou Ann talking to her like one of her kindergarten students, but she let it go as she always did. "I want to talk to Howard. He's the one who ran the CT and the MRI, so he'd have more of an idea as to what's going on inside her head."

"Isn't this the miracle you prayed for gra'ma?" Lexi dumped a heavy load of syrup on her pancakes, eyeing her plate with great anticipation.

"That's enough sweetie." Keith quickly retrieved the syrup bottle from her. "Save some for daddy."

Lou Ann pushed her honey colored hair behind both ears. Then picked up Lexi's fork to cut up the pancakes and sausage for her.

"I guess it is Lexi. I just want to make sure there's nothing wrong."

"God doesn't make bad miracles, does he?" Lexi tilted her pixie blond head and squinted at her grandmother through confused blue eyes.

"No he doesn't. Thank you for reminding me of that." Peggy took a deep breath to thoughtfully absorb Lexi's comment. Wishfully she wanted to see things through the trusting eyes of her granddaughter. Yet there was too many questions in her mind shadowed by doubt and even fear.

"That's enough questions dear," Lou Ann held the fork up in front of Lexi once she finished cutting up the pancakes. "you need to eat now, okay?"

The little girl took the fork. Eagerly she began shoveling in huge mouthfuls of the sweet warm cakes. Syrup dripped from her chin as she shoveled in more.

Peggy had to giggle at the girl's enthusiasm. It reminded her of when her children were that age. "You know...it could go back to Eve's childhood memories somehow. I think she was around Lexi's age when she told me about some man named Hamlet, Hamuel or something like that, being in her room one night when she woke up from a terrible dream. I tried to assure her that no one could have gotten in the house. Yet she kept insisting that he was there. She said his shirt smelled like Mrs. O'Leary's flower garden after a spring rain. And that when he put his arm around her shoulders it was as warm as sunshine."

"I remember something about that too." Keith thoughtfully dabbed the coffee from his mustache with his napkin. "She kept asking Troy and I if we were in her room." He chuckled at the memory. "I remember because she asked if one of us had put on a shirt fresh from the dryer before coming into her room."

"Yes," Peggy nodded and ran a hand through her short hair. "She thought one of you were playing a trick on her, until I finally convinced her that no one could have gotten in the house and that I would have heard one of you boys walking around." She added before taking another bite of her eggs.

"She could be having some type of flash back or dementia. I suppose it would be confusing to finally see after being blind for thirty years. The nurse that called the house said that she was found wandering the halls, holding her head and mumbling something about a nightmare, and that she requested an aspirin." Keith injected. He was only a physical therapist, but he had learned a little here and there, from his dad and from working at the hospital for twelve years. "There could even be some burned tissue in her optical nerves from the intense amount of electricity that bolted through her. It could have formed spots or shadows on her retinas to make her think she was seeing something. We'll have to see what the doctor's say."

"I would've believed her, just like I believe her now." Lexi concurred, syrup still running down her tiny chin. "Don't you believe her mommy? You used to tell me there were angels watching over me. Don't they watch over Auntie Eve too?" The more excited she got the faster she talked.

With a responding nod, Lou Ann dipped her napkin into her ice water, and cleaned up the sticky mess around Lexi's mouth and hands. Lexi shivered at the cold water, but she let her mother clean her up, she was too keen on being clean to complain. Plus she'd take the ice water over a tongue-moistened napkin any day.

Once they all finished their food and their second cups of coffee, they were about to go back up to Eve's room, when Howard entered the cafeteria. He headed straight to their table once he spotted them.

Dr. Bowman informed them that Dr. Booker would be doing three or four other tests, and since Booker was the eye specialist they needed to consult him. He said it was possible her retinas were simply having a hard time adjusting to the job of focusing. He also added that there might be refraction errors in the cornea, which might cause her to see things that weren't there. Bowman finished by telling them that the MRI and CT scans both appeared normal, and that there was no hematoma or edema to the brain.

When they met with Booker outside Eve's room, he confirmed what Bowman had said, then he informed the nurses station to bring Eve down for more tests after she finished her breakfast. "Her eyes have never had to focus and comprehend before, so there will be some adjustment for her there. I'm also going to closely examine her peripheral vision. There may even be floaters that are causing her to think she's seeing something."

Peggy felt a little better after talking with the doctors, but she was still concerned that there could be some underlying problem with Eve's newly found vision. Maybe it was just too good to be true. Or too hard to imagine God actually giving them this miracle, even as much as she wanted to believe it. She just didn't want Eve to be disappointed if the miracle didn't last. This was the greatest thing Peggy had ever experienced, yet she was afraid to be too happy too soon, not wanting to embrace another disappointment for her daughter or herself.

Chapter 6

"What day is it?" Eve asked the nurse pushing her wheelchair down the hallway.

"It's Friday, the 4th of July dear. So if you look out your window tonight you should be able to see the fireworks display." The nurse wheeled her into the room for her eye exam.

"Is it really necessary for me to be pushed around in this? I can walk just fine you know." Eve was used to taking care of herself, even in her blindness she liked doing as much as possible on her own. She had never been one to cower from a challenge, quite the opposite in fact, she had always risen up to meet it head on.

"It's just hospital policy. Besides, when you leave here with dilated pupils, you'll be glad to have someone push you back to your room." The nurse steadied the wheelchair while Eve got out and settled into the exam chair. "Dr. Booker will be in shortly."

"I'm here...I'm here." Booker called out as he walked through the door slightly out of breath, hands raised in the air.

Eve turned towards the familiar voice. Seeing the face of Curtis T. Booker for the first time in the five years she'd known him. "Boy, that was shortly." She proclaimed as she took in the sight of him. He looked younger than she had imagined, in fact, he didn't look much older than her. He had light brown hair and pale blue eyes. Short and stocky. "I hope you're here to tell me when I can go home. No one else seems to want to give me the okay."

"You should be able to go home tomorrow. If we don't find anything on these tests I'm about to run." Curtis assured her with a warm smile as he pulled a chair over to sit in front of her. "I made up a Braille chart just for you, since that's all you know how to read right now."

Eve said a silent prayer under her breath, then she settled back in her chair to ready herself for the exams.

First he assessed her visual acuity by having her read off the Braille letters on the chart. Then he checked her visual fields. Next he put a slit-lamp in front of her to measure her intraocular pressure. Finally he dilated her pupils for the ophthalmoscopy. Examining the cornea, lens, vitreous humor, and the vessels at the back of the eye.

After two hours of tests and small talk, Eve was given an *all's fine*, and taken back to her room. What she didn't understand is why they were making her stay in the hospital another night. If everything was *fine*, why couldn't she just go home? Booker explained how they wanted to keep an eye on her one more night.

Her family was all waiting in her room when she returned. Even Aunt Maggy and Uncle Alex were there. Eve was quick to search Maggy's eyes to find the light, and was relieved when she saw it. And they were all relieved to hear that Eve's entire exam turned out normal, and that she'd be able to check out in the morning. Keith had to leave to get to work, but everyone else visited with Eve until dinner, then they left so she could rest after eating.

After finding out who had come to see her while she was in the coma, Eve's mind was too busy thinking to rest. Nearly all of the church congregation and all of her friends from the courthouse, including Adam Webber, an attorney she barely knew. Adam had asked her out to lunch a few times, but she had always made an excuse not to go. Not that she thought there was anything wrong with him. She just had issues about going anywhere alone with a man she hardly knew. In fact, she only dated two guys in her entire life, a one time date to her high school prom, and then she dated a guy from her church for a month. Both ended on a sour note.

Her mother also said that Adam had brought in a big bouquet of yellow roses, which died along with all the other flowers before Eve came out of the coma. Her mother read all the cards to her that had came with her flowers. Which made Eve realize that she needed to learn to read regular writing. There were a lot of things to learn now that she could see.

Once she finished eating she got out of bed to look out the window to see if Hamuel was still out on the ledge. He had been out there all day, ever since her family arrived, as if he were giving them some privacy. She wanted to ask Hamuel why she hadn't seen her mother's angel, among other questions. So she tapped on the window to get his attention, then motioned for him to come into the room. When he did, her first question was about her mother's angel,

"I saw the light in my mother's eyes, but where was her angel?"

"He waited and watched from the roof top. That is where we often watch over you from." He crossed his arms over his wide chest and sat in the chair next to her bed. He watched her pace the room while she thought out her next question.

"Is that where my brother's angel was? Or does he have one? I know I didn't see the light in his eyes, but..." She shot a helpless look towards Hamuel as her eyes filled with fret. She couldn't bear the thought of her brother not being under God's protection, especially when he wasn't walking in the light.

"There is an angel that watches over their family."

"As in just one angel for all three of them?" She ran a hand through her thick cinnamon hair and proceeded to pace after Hamuel confirmed with a nod. She knew that wasn't good, since one angel could only be one place at a time. So not everyone would be protected at all times. "So who does the angel stay with the most?"

"The child of course." He looked at her like that was something she should have known without asking. "Unless there is a special prayer of protection on one of them."

"I'm not sure I can handle knowing some of these things. It's a burden on my heart to know that my brother isn't in God's light. I'm not so sure I can handle this gift I've been given."

"If it was something you could not handle, then God would not have given it to you. For only he knows what you can and can not handle. For that reason he chose you. It would have been even more overwhelming for someone who was not blind to see these things. But since you saw nothing before, this is not such a shock for you to see now. The human brain can store 100 trillion facts and can handle 15 thousand decisions a second, so you will learn to *handle* your new gift, as long as it lasts." He emphasized to help her get the message clearly.

But it was his last five words that stopped Eve from pacing. "You mean this is all going to end? It's not permanent? I could be blind again?"

"All I have been told is that the gift was for a time. I do not know how long. I do think you will be able to keep your natural sight, but perhaps not the spiritual sight. For this reason," He held up his hands in a jester of helplessness, "God does not want you to focus on *me* or any other spirits, unless it is *his* Holy Spirit. He wants you to look to him for all things. And as long as you can see and speak to me, you will tend to look to me for answers, just as you are doing now. Which, by the way, you should limit speaking to other angels, and you should *never* speak to the dark angels. The dark angels will surely deceive you, for the truth is not in them, just as the light is not in them."

Eve could see his point and got the impression that he didn't want her asking too many questions. She still had several questions, but she chose not to ask him, at least not until nightfall. Then when the fireworks display began flashing across the darkening skyline, she asked him to teach her the colors. It was a delight to her eyes to finally see the very thing that used to startle her as a child.

Near the end of the fireworks display Eve saw something else that startled her. An angel jumped out of a window from another room. As he did, his white jacket blew open and transformed into a pair of wings. Underneath his jacket was a brilliant golden chest plate that gleamed as if the sun were shining upon it. As he raised his left arm a golden shield instantly appeared. Her gaze followed his right hand as he reached for a sword at his side. When he pulled it from the sheath the blade was such pure silver that it flashed like a bolt of lightening against the darkness.

Her eyes continued to follow his decent. Then she finally caught sight of what he was chasing, when the dark spirit turned to fight. The dark spirit drew his sword and swung wildly at the angel of light. Sparks flew as the two blades collided, again and again. The dark spirit was pushed backwards each time the angel delivered his powerful blows.

The dark spirit turned to flee once again. The angel swung his blade one last time and it connected with the dark spirits arm, sending him tumbling downward like a gymnast rolling on a mat. Blood running bright red down his slate gray arm. After a brief but quick descending spiral the dark spirit hit the ground running then suddenly jetted back into the sky like a shooting star, and was instantly gone. The angel didn't chase him, but instead let him escape to tend to his wound.

Eve had been speechless after witnessing the spirits battle. It was all she could do to crawl into bed, pull the covers up to her chin, and lay there until she fell asleep. She was full of questions, but instead of asking Hamuel she prayed silently for the answers.

She was thankful the next morning to be released. Seeing the city pass by through the window of Keith's mini van kept her eyes busy. The buildings and trees were nothing like she'd imagined them to be. Now there were colors and dimensions to the world around her, as well as spirits everywhere, she

Unseen

even saw one riding on the roof of an ambulance that was speeding back to the hospital, so she said a silent prayer for the passenger inside.

Keith shook his head and chuckled. His eyes gleamed with amusement as he watched Eve gazing through the window with such excitement. "I'll bet if I rolled down your window you'd have your head and tongue hanging out like a puppy."

"This is so exciting and new." Eve beamed as she continued to stare out the window. "Speaking of dogs, how's mine been doing?"

"Shadow is just fine, other than missing you of course. She didn't eat very well the first few weeks you were in the hospital."

Eve could hardly wait to see her best friend and companion. Not to mention, to finally see what a chocolate brown Labrador really looked like. Her Aunt Maggy had given her the dog ten years ago after having it trained to be a guide dog. Her disastrous senior prom date is what stemmed the whole idea of Eve getting a guide dog. For protection more so than guidance.

Eve wondered why no one else had come with Keith to pick her up from the hospital, but she was too busy looking around to ask.

Keith drove straight down Central, pointing out Sacred Heart Academy as they drove past. Eve stared at the school as memories flashed through her mind.

Unseen

Faceless teachers identified only by their voices and distinguishing perfumes. That's where she learned that the nose could smell up to 10 thousand different odors. And that her touch was sensitive enough to detect an item 1/25,000th of an inch thick. And her tongue could taste one part of quinine in two million parts of water. Along with learning Braille, Spanish and anything else she wanted to learn. She was stunned to see a spiritual battle take place on the rooftop of the school.

Keith turned when they reached Spruce Street. It was a brick street, so the familiar sound the tires made told Eve she was nearly home.

Keith pointed out a three-story tan brick building and told her it was the courthouse. She saw yet two more battles taking place in the sky above the courthouse. He drove to the end of the block and slowed down by the house, but he quickly realized that she wasn't going to recognize the place by sight. It wasn't until he pulled into the driveway that she looked at him in question. Knowing her question, he simply gave her a confirmation nod, and a thin smile.

Shadow gave Eve a warm welcome when they entered the privacy fence to the back yard. Eve kneeled down and hugged the dog as it licked her face. "It's good to see you too girl." Eve stroked the dog's thick short hair. Shadow whimpered, as if saying the same thing. As Eve glanced up at the gray two-story house she saw Hamuel sitting with a couple other angels on the peak of the roof.

Keith lifted Eve up by her elbow. "Better go say hi to mom too."

Eve drew her brows together wondering why he seemed in a hurry for her to get inside. Her silent question was answered as they stepped inside the back door to the kitchen and a room full of people yelled "Surprise."

Since Eve didn't yet recognize people by sight she walked around to each person and asked them to speak, then she knew their name from their voice, thanking them for being there. She also found herself looking into each ones eyes to see if there was any light within them.

Co-workers, church members, neighbors, even the police chief Harry Crow was there. And last but not least, Adam Webber was there. The attorney who was years younger and way more handsome than Eve had guessed. Most of the other attorneys were over fifty, so she had never asked Adam how old he was, she simply assumed. Obviously a very bad presumption.

Now that she could see him, she guessed him to be closer to his mid-thirties. He had sandy brown hair that was streaked on top with blond highlights. It was short and parted to the right. His eyes were sky blue like Hamuel's, only the light of Christ was not in them. His deep tanned features made his white teeth seem even brighter. His T-shirt and jeans defined his slim muscular frame all too well. He stood five inches over her as she hugged him and thanked him for coming.

"I wouldn't have missed it for the world." His sultry reply made the hairs at the nap of her neck dance. It was unnerving how his voice had such a strange affect on her from day one, and still counting.

Chapter 7

Adam stepped outside to get the Sunday paper as soon as he heard his parent's car leave the house. He always liked to read it before his dad got a hold of it, since his dad left it in such a mess, so Adam would slip out and get it after they left for church.

Splashed all over the front page was, "2 Murders in 1 Night," the headlines read. As Adam read the article, it appeared there was a death caused by a drunk driver on the same night his new client was touching evidence at her own crime scene. A seventeen year-old girl, Mandy Daubs, and a twenty-one year-old ranch hand, Lisa Bixbee, both died that night according to the article.

Unseen

Adam leafed through the pages to see if there was anything on Evelyn Kincaid and her miracle healing. He hoped there would be something, since the reporters had came in and crashed her homecoming party just to get an interview from her. Adam finally found a small article. It briefly explained how she was struck by lightning, in a coma for forty days, then how her sight was restored when she woke up, and how it had baffled the doctors. Adam did discover that her blindness had been due to an unexplainable functional disorder, and how everything there was normal, it simply didn't function. Her eyes simply hadn't sent signals to the nerve endings to produce an image on the retina, until after the lightning strike.

Adam looked down at his black and white Australian Shepherd curled up on the floor. "Why doesn't good news ever hit the front page?" Patch lifted his head and barked as if he would like to answer, but the language barrier was unbreakable. Then the dog just watched Adam through his pale blue, almost white eyes, waiting for a piece of bacon. "Yah, you know what I'm talking about, don't ya boy?" The dog wagged his stubby bobtail in response.

Adam turned his attention back to his coffee and newspaper. Reading the obituaries next, although he couldn't think why, it was just more depressing news. Yet when he saw the name, he knew what had drawn him there, Lisa Bixbee. From the black and white photo he could see how pretty she was, but the newspaper print gave no indication of hair or eye color. It was easy to see the truth in what Rachel had said about Bret flirting with them both, since they were both very attractive young girls. Plus from what Adam knew about Bret, he knew Bret as a womanizer all the way through high school. Mandy Daubs was another nice looking young girl who should have had a long life in front of her.

Gun shot to the abdomen. That meant Lisa had nearly bled out by the time she reached the hospital, only to die somewhere between the ambulance and ER.

Adam couldn't help but wonder if she had been able to speak to anyone during that time period. Could she have given one of the EMS workers the name of her killer? Or had she been unconscious the whole time? That was something he'd have to find out. If he wanted to clear Rachel's name he'd need more than just her word to do it with.

Without wasting another minute Adam was on the phone to the hospital. He got the names of everyone working the EMS unit and ER that night. Then Monday he'd check with the detective on the case to see if they had interviewed any of them yet. Adam knew detective George Dixon from high school, so he knew he'd be straight with him.

Chapter 8

It had taken Eve a long time to get to sleep only to wake up just before dawn. She not only wanted to see the sun rise for the second time in her life, but she was anxious to go to church and give thanks to God for her sight. Her pastor, Rev. Brace, was at her home coming party and he had asked her to give testimony to the miracle that God had performed.

Full of excitement Eve was quick to shower and dress. Then she rushed into the kitchen to make breakfast, since she hadn't heard her mother come down stairs yet, she knew she was the first one up. Peggy's bedroom was upstairs along with a small sitting room. While Eve's bedroom was downstairs along with the bathroom, living room and kitchen.

After both boys had moved out their bedroom was converted into a dining room.

Eve's grandparents on her father's side both died before she was born. In their will they left the house to Charles, since he was their only child. Charles couldn't bring himself to sell the place, so they moved in. Then when Eve was born blind, they made a decision never to move, that way she could grow up in a familiar environment.

Eve paused for a moment to look at the window over the sink. It had long since been replaced. Like the memory of that night. Due to her impact against the floor, all she remembered was standing there to get some water. Then her next memory is waking up in the hospital. So she didn't recall the feeling of being struck by lightning, and the glass crashing in around her. Brushing off the thought like shards of glass in a dustpan, she walked to the fridge and got out the eggs, then began making breakfast.

Eve still arranged the food on her plate in a clockwise manor, bacon at two o'clock, eggs at six o'clock and toast at ten o'clock. It was a habit she didn't imagine she'd change now just because she could see. She even found herself still putting a finger in her glass to feel when the milk was at the top.

The church bus came to pick them up as usual. The only difference was neither of them had their canes with them this time, and Shadow stayed behind as well. Peggy was getting around much better since she'd begun taking her medicine regularly, so now she didn't need her cane anymore than Eve needed hers. Eve prayed both canes could be permanently stored in the closet.

Eve's eyes were busy viewing both sides of the six and a half block drive to church. She noticed some cars being followed by angels and a few rooftops with angels standing watch. But one thing she wasn't quite prepared for, was the circle of angels that loomed over the church roof, adorning it like a phosphorescent halo. The steeple towered above the luminous sea of angels like a lighthouse.

Her heart flooded with joy at the sight and her eyes turned to pools of sea green mist. She longed to tell her mother what she was seeing, but she didn't dare, since she knew her mother wouldn't believe her anyway. She'd just have to pray hard that someday she could convince her.

"I think soon I'll be able to drive us again myself" Peggy leaned over to whisper so that Eve was the only one to hear.

"I need to learn to drive, among other things, like reading real words." Eve whispered back as they got up to exit the van.

Mrs. Chadwick was the first one to welcome them. Eve's heart sank when she saw no light in the older lady's eyes. She prayed that the disappointment in her heart didn't show on her face. It was stunning to see such a faithful member without the light in them, especially someone so giving. Eve was glad she only saw three darkened eyes out of the people who greeted her. Anymore than that and she might have broke out crying right there.

"*Please God, give me some encouraging words to warm those cold spirits in here.*" Eve prayed in her mind as she walked to the front of the church to give her testimony. Looking back over the pews of people the church suddenly seemed huge. There must have been close to two hundred people staring at her. The high vaulted ceiling seemed to rise even higher as her pulse surged through her veins and shortened her breath.

She swallowed back the lump and prayed for courage. "As most of you know, I used to be blind, but God chose to be gracious enough to make me a miracle in your sight." She giggled into the microphone, mostly from nervousness. "And mine as well. I don't know yet why he chose to heal me, maybe so I could tell others how God does still heal people. God is the same as he was two thousand years ago. Jesus healed the blind then with a simple touch, but he chose to heal me through a different touch of his divine power, a flash of lightning."

A sudden calmness washed over her as a scripture came to her mind. "It makes me think of John 9 verse 5 when Jesus said, 'While I am in the world, I am the light of the world.' We need to be that light in the world today. It's our turn to shine for Christ in this darkened world. Thank you all for the prayers and the cards." Eve walked quickly back to her seat as everyone clapped. She didn't like the attention, but she hoped her words were encouraging.

Peggy exhaled in relief at the way Eve handle the situation. She was so glad Eve hadn't said anything in front of the whole church about being able to see angels. She had hoped she wouldn't take her little joke that far and embarrass her in front of everyone. Peggy had almost forgotten about it, until today, because Eve hadn't mentioned it again since the hospital.

When they began singing Amazing Grace tears streamed down Eve's cheeks. Now those words, '*I once was blind but now I see*', had a more personal heartfelt meaning. Even her mother seemed touched by it, since she reached out to hold Eve's hand until the song had ended.

Unseen

The following morning Peggy protested when Eve got dressed and ready for work. Peggy wanted her to take another week off, but Eve didn't see any reason she couldn't return to work. She didn't want to sit around the house being bored, and she felt like she'd already had plenty of time off work, and more than enough bed rest. They were both being stubborn, but Eve won the battle when she mentioned the fact that she didn't want to lose her job by missing any more days.

The walk down the sidewalk and across the street put a smile on Eve's face. It was nice to be able to see the honeysuckle she smelled as she walked past it. Shadow didn't like being left at home, but it wasn't necessary for her to go with her now.

She stopped in front of the courthouse doors and looked up at the structure. Two pillars on each side reached up to greet the peak over the doors. Large tan bricks formed the three-story building from the ground up. The green and white tile flooring caught her eye as she entered. She stared at the beautiful pattern of colors. Then her eyes moved up the walls that were marble half way up, to the intricate sculptured moldings along the ceiling, and then to the large dome shaped light fixtures. She never realized how much beauty and craftsmanship she had missed in the seven years she'd worked there.

Eve finally made her way to the elevator that would take her up to her office.

When Maggy turned to see Eve standing in the doorway, a bright smile parted her red lips. "Oh sugar, I didn't realize you'd be back to work today or I wouldn't have bothered coming in." Maggy crossed the small office to give Eve a hug. "I should have guessed you wouldn't be able to stay at home and do nothing."

Eve smiled and smoothed her hair back towards the bun it was neatly wrapped in. "Yah, you know me. I like to stay busy." She laid her brief case on the desk. "I'm glad you're here though. I'd like to ask you something."

"Anything sugar, just ask." Maggy pulled up a chair for Eve to sit on, then another one facing it for her.

"Since you have more patience than mom, I was wondering if you could teach me how to drive and read regular words."

"Sure I can. But the reading might be better taught by one of the teachers from Sacred Heart Academy." Maggy's auburn dyed hair was barely long enough to stay behind her ear when she tucked it there.

"I'd rather you taught me. It's not like I can't already read, I just read in Braille." Eve's green eyes pleaded with her Aunt. Eve wanted to talk to her about seeing into the spiritual realm too, but she wasn't sure she should just yet. Although she was sure her mother had already mentioned it to her, since Maggy was the only living relative Peggy had left.

"Okay. I'll be back after work today to pick you up and we'll get started driving in the field at my place." Maggy smiled and patted Eve's shoulder. "How's that sound sweetie?"

"Great." Eve smiled back. That would give her the rest of the day to think about how to bring up the spiritual matter. She desperately needed to talk and to find someone besides a six-year-old who believed her.

The rest of Eve's day wasn't as easy to get through. She had a lot of straightening up to do in her office. Then she had four hearings scheduled to report which were domestic cases and misdemeanors.

Since Maggy had been filling in for Eve while she was in the hospital, Eve had to take her own stenography machine back into the courtroom to get it set up before court opened. Eve had a special steno machine that printed in Braille so she'd be able to read what she transcribed.

When she stepped into the courtroom, she immediately looked up at the high ceiling. She always knew the room sounded huge from the sound of the voices, but now she could see just how large.

She looked around to see if Hamuel was inside with her, since she could easily see him fitting into the oversized room, but he wasn't. Instead the walls were lined with pictures of all the past judges; at least that's what the bailiff had once told her.

Hamuel didn't show up until the cases were presented to the judge. Which was also when all the other spirits showed up, both good and evil.

By the end of the week Eve found herself actually closing her eyes at times, while she was reporting, just so she could concentrate without the spirits in the room distracting her. Between the challenge of concentrating in the courtroom and learning to drive, it turned into a long exhausting two weeks for Eve.

Fortunately the spirits didn't fight in the courtroom, but on occasion Eve did see a dark spirit poking his fingers into the minds of those he was tormenting. According to Hamuel, the dark spirits could only make that type of contact with non believers, and it happened more often when there were no prayers going up for that person.

She did manage to talk to her Aunt about her gifted sight one evening while driving through the field at Maggy's farm. Maggy made no comment at that time, but she seemed to believe her. She also told Eve that she'd have to give Peggy more time to be able to believe. Peggy was a year older, so she was more prone to be cautious and protective, which is why it took her longer to accept things; according to Maggy.

Chapter 9

After three weeks of driving, reading, and dealing with spirits in the courtroom, Eve was exhausted and looking forward to a quiet weekend at home. Only when she got home Friday evening she discovered her brother Troy and his wife Debbie had drove in from Wichita.

"Hey, little sister we came to see how you're doing." Troy flashed a thin boyish smile at her as she entered the back door. He was the oldest sibling at thirty-seven, but with a clean-shaven face, and his deep red hair he could have passed as the youngest. Especially since he still had a few of his boy-hood freckles lingering on his cheeks.

"Don't you mean you came so I could *see* you?" She giggled at her little play on words. It was the only way she could keep the disappointment from her face, since she saw no light flickering in his hazel eyes. She hugged him then stepped into the house and looked around the kitchen to see if Debbie had come with him. Debbie was sitting at the dining room table with Peggy drinking tea.

Eve walked over to hug her sister-in-law. She felt a little awkward since she had never really gotten to know Debbie very well, never the less, when Debbie stood in greeting, she hugged her. Debbie and Troy had been married for seven years, but four of those years they hadn't come around at all. Her heart sank lower when she noticed no light in Debbie's eyes either. She knew Debbie was a believer from what her mother had said. In fact, her mother had said that Debbie was always trying to get Troy to attend church more often, but their schedules were just too demanding.

"It's such wonderful news that you can see. Have the doctors figured out how the lightning corrected the problem?" Debbie's dark brown eyes darted back and forth into Eve's eyes, as if she were looking for something. Debbie was only three inches taller, but she must have thought she was a lot taller, because she lowered her head to look Eve square in the face.

Debbie had dark shoulder length hair, almost as dark as Keith's. She was thin and well shaped, and from what Eve was told, Debbie came from a very wealthy family. Which was apparent in her mannerism, from her speech and sophisticated movements, to her neatly pressed designer clothes.

"No more wonderful than the God that granted me this miracle." Eve's mouth curled up on one side. She liked it when she got an opportunity to brag about God's goodness. Especially to those walking in darkness.

Eve went to the fridge and got out the tea to make herself a glass. While she had the pitcher out she offered everyone else a refill. When she got to her mom's glass, Peggy informed her, that Keith and his family would be meeting them for dinner at the Brushfire restaurant around six. Eve knew there was little hope of getting to bed early, but it would be worth it to spend some time with her whole family.

Eve couldn't help but notice Adam at the restaurant. Especially since he was sitting with a woman just three tables over from theirs. As hard as she tried, she couldn't stop her mind from wondering who the woman was. Was it someone he was dating or perhaps a sister? Maybe a client? Somewhere deep inside her, she hoped for one of the latter, although she wasn't exactly sure why.

Adam did hold up a hand to acknowledge Eve when they stood to leave the restaurant. He was wearing one of the gray business suits Eve had seen him in a number of times. The lady with him, however, was wearing a bright pink strapless dress that showed too much skin for Eve's liking.

Peggy turned to look when she saw Eve wave back. "Isn't that Adam Webber?" She turned back for Eve's reply. When Eve nodded to confirm, Peggy went on to say, "He seemed very concerned about you when he came to the hospital to see you. How well do you know the man?"

Eve gave a slight shrug. "Not very well at all really. We've talked at the courthouse a few times, but that's about it."

"Adam Webber. I think I went to school with him." Troy added in his two cents to the conversation. "In fact, I know I did. He was one of the jocks, a basketball player that hung out with George Dixon all the way through high school."

"He's an attorney, so it's just a working relationship, if you could really even call it that." Eve moved the food on her plate with her fork and tried to change the subject. "This is wonderful chicken. You guys should have tried some."

"And I hear that Dixon is a detective on the police force. I guess that just goes to show you should never stereotype people. Back then we always assumed that the jocks were more bronze than brains and that they'd never amount to much in the career field." Troy cut off another chunk of his steak to shovel it in his mouth.

"He seemed more concerned than a mere acquaintance when I spoke with him in the hospital." Peggy went on. "A mere acquaintance wouldn't go to the expense of bringing you a dozen yellow roses."

"He is nice looking. Wouldn't you agree?" Lou Ann commented over the rim of her tea glass before taking a drink. Her eyes studied Eve intently for the slightest reaction. Her eyes left for only a second when she saw Debbie nod in agreement with her statement.

"And what are you doing noticing his looks?" Keith questioned his wife, but Lou Ann simply waved off his comment with a hand and pursed lips.

"I guess so." Eve shrugged it off, wishing they would all drop the subject. "And it looks like he's already dating someone, so will you all please stop trying to be match makers."

"No one said anything about match making." Peggy informed her, in a matter of fact tone. "Is that what you had in mind dear?"

Eve gave her a look that clearly said, '*drop the subject*'. Then she tried to gain interest in her chicken again, but her appetite seemed to have left with Adam.

"It has been around ten years since you've even dated anyone hasn't it?" Keith questioned, hanging onto the obviously touchy subject.

"Nine," Eve corrected. "If you want an exact count. But then who's been counting?"

Keith and Troy both broke out laughing. Then Troy added. "Obviously you have been, since you're the one who knows the *exact count*."

"You guys shouldn't tease Auntie like that," Lexi scolded with a small finger wiggling in the air. "It's not nice. What does she want with a yucky boy anyway?"

There was another round of soft laughter, but they did finally let up on Eve, and dropped the subject.

Eve was thankful that someone took up for her, so she gave Lexi a smile of gratitude, along with a promise for dessert. The two shared a deep admiration for one another. An unbreakable bond.

That's when Eve turned her attention to the fact that Troy and Debbie didn't have any children yet. So she got them all on a subject that didn't involve her in anyway, other than to be the adoring Auntie when they had a child. Only Eve knew she'd never see their children as often as she saw Lexi. But that was okay with her, since she didn't want anyone to over shadow her attentions on Lexi.

It turned into an exhausting weekend. Especially since Eve tried so hard to convince her brother's they needed to get back into church. Saturday night Eve prayed and searched through her Bible until she fell asleep. Then she tried even harder in the morning to get Troy and Debbie to stay a few more hours and go to church with them. Only Troy had his mind made up, as Kincaid's had a tendency to do, and a snowstorm in July wouldn't have stopped him from leaving.

The only hope Eve got was when Troy said he would start looking for a church in Wichita the following weekend. Debbie said she'd make him hold to his word, since she had wanted to do that for a long time herself, but simply hadn't.

Chapter 10

$\mathcal{I}$n the middle of the following week, just when Eve thought she was getting back into the hang of things, a DUI arraignment threw her a curve ball. What caught Eve's attention first was the dark spirits that came into the courtroom. Eve recognized them from the hospital rooftop. They were the two spirits that had been talking about the soul they were tormenting with alcohol. So Adam's client, Darwin Talbot, was the man they were tormenting.

The bailiff, Matt Masters, announced the entry of the judge, Diane L. Knapp. A beautiful blonde in her early to mid-forties she was the youngest judge on the bench, but she knew her laws right down to every exclamation mark.

"The State v. Darwin A. Talbot on the charge of negligent homicide. Docket number... Case number..."

Eve's fingers typed out the numbers that the clerk read off, but her eyes were on the couple ambling into the courtroom. An angel followed the couple holding a small gold vase. They found some empty seats behind the district attorney's table. Then Hamuel instantly appeared next to the other angel. She could see the two angels talking, but she couldn't hear anything.

The district attorney, Victor Dillon, stood, buttoned his jacket and adjusted his tie before speaking. Dillon was in his late fifties, balding and overweight, but he knew the law inside and out. "On the night of July 3rd around eleven thirty P.M...."

Hearing the date, Eve knew she'd assumed correctly about Talbot.

Eve noticed when the woman began sobbing against her husband's shoulder, the angel behind them held up the vase, and began pouring something over their heads. It looked like stardust or an extra fine grain of silver glitter. An endless supply poured from the small vase. Eve focused back on listening, but she couldn't stop wondering what the angels were discussing, and what was being poured from the vase.

Dillon did his usual pacing back and forth in front of his table. It was a wonder the tiles weren't worn away in the floor. Even when Eve couldn't see his pacing, she'd heard plenty of it over the years. "Mr. Talbot was driving while under the influence of alcohol when he crashed into the drivers' side of Mandy Daubs car. Ms. Daubs died at the scene as a result of this accident…"

Eve's fingers kept pounding out every word Dillon spoke on her steno machine, but her eyes drifted back to the sobbing woman. The angel tipped the vase higher as the woman cried harder. Then it dawned on her; the elderly couple must be the parents of the victim.

"…If Mr. Talbot had not been intoxicated this most likely could have been avoided. But Talbot's blood alcohol levels were clearly well above the legal limits." Dillon took a piece of paper from his opened briefcase. He approached the bench with the papers that showed Talbot's Breathalyzer test.

Eve typed out the level of intoxication as Dillon quoted it to Judge Knapp. Diane looked over the paperwork, then handed it back to Dillon.

"At the point of impact Talbot's speed was estimated to be fifty-five miles per hour. Which is yet another violation, since the speed zone in that area of town is only thirty-five miles per hour." Dillon crossed one arm over his chest to prop his other arm up to rub his chin in thought, not missing a single stride in his boundless pacing. "There was no indication that Talbot even tried to stop. No brake marks were left on the street at the scene. Which is yet another violation, since there is a stop sign at that intersection in the direction Talbot was traveling. Clearly a gross neglect of vehicular operation if there ever was one. So much so, that Talbot nearly lost his own life, since he himself was admitted to the hospital that very night."

Dillon's pacing finally lead him back around the table to his seat. "I have nothing further to add at this point your honor." Then, unbuttoning his jacket, he took his seat.

Judge Knapp turned her blue eyes towards the defendant's attorney, Adam Webber. "What would you like to add on your client's behalf Mr. Webber?"

Adam stood and smoothed down his navy blue jacket. Then he gestured helplessly with his hands. "My client would like to enter a plea of guilty."

Eve looked the defendant over for the first time. His face was pale, which made his puffy eyes appear even redder. It was clear that the man had not slept well since the accident. Regret was more than evident in the man's face.

Adam walked around in front of his table, leaning back against it he crossed his feet in a very relaxed manner. "Mr. Talbot is well aware of the pain and suffering he has caused and he is ready to accept whatever punishment the court deems fit. I motion for the court to lessen the charge to involuntary manslaughter, since my client had no intent to harm anyone, least of all a seventeen year old girl. My client has two children of his own and sympathizes deeply with the parents of Ms. Daubs. Mr. Talbot has shown great remorse for his negligence." Adam made another helpless gesture with his hands. "That's all I have at this time your honor."

Knapp glanced down at her watch to check the time. "Very well. I'll call a recess for lunch to make my decision." She added as she stood and requested all to rise. "Court will re-adjourn in one hour."

Eve looked over to see if Hamuel was going to follow her out of the room, since she had a few gnawing questions for him. Hamuel must have read the anxiety in her eyes, because he vanished with the blink of an eye. Eve was getting used to his quick appearances by now, so she knew he'd be in her office already.

She didn't even think to close her office door before the words were out of her mouth upon entering. "What was that all about? The vase I mean." Her green eyes studied him closely.

"Ishibah was pouring comfort out upon them. The prayers with their church family are strong, so the comfort has been endlessly pouring out since the accident." Hamuel informed as he looked out the window to the street below.

"Why did that girl have to die so young?" Eve sank down into her desk chair and dropped her head into her hands. "She had her whole life ahead of her."

"She enlarged the Creator's kingdom greatly in her seventeen year ministry and her final purpose was to die. Don't you see?" Hamuel turned away from the window to look at Eve. "Her death was the only thing that could humble Darwin and bring him to his knees. Two nights ago he turned his life back over to God, because he knew that was the only way to find forgiveness. Didn't you see the light in his eyes?"

"Really? I didn't think to look in his eyes." She looked up shaking her head. "Couldn't there have been another way?"

Hamuel shook his head no. "Just as there was no other way, than for Christ to lay down his life."

"Girl, if you're going to talk to yourself, you should at least shut the door." Venus stepped through the door wearing a bright grin, followed by a short giggle. "I know you're crazy, but are you sure you want everyone else to know it?" They giggled together at her comment. "I'm going to have to pass on lunch today. I just got a call from the daycare and

I've got to go pick up my son and take him to my mom's. The stuffy nose he had this morning seems to have gotten worse."

Eve and Venus had been good friends for five years, since they met, which was two weeks after Venus became the county clerk. They joked around a lot to help each other get through the day. Eve hadn't even known Venus was black until she saw her at her home coming party, not that the color of her skin mattered anyway – then or now. They also had a standing luncheon together everyday since they met, unless something came up, like now.

"Okay, tomorrow then. Take care of your son and I'll keep him in my prayers."

"Thanks." Venus turned to leave, but Adam Webber's frame was filling the doorway. "Oh, pardon me." She giggled again shyly.

"No, pardon me." Adam stepped to the side so she could pass. "Sounds like you're free for lunch." Adam offered a charming smile to Eve. "If a man asked you to lunch for a fourth time, would you turn him down again?"

As always a tingle danced down her spin from the smooth sultry sound of his voice when he spoke directly to her. Only this time it was like a double whammy, since she could see his attractive smile now. Eve's face reddened with a blushing smile. "I guess that would depend on who the man was."

Adam walked further into the room until he was standing in front of her desk staring down at her. "You mean there's others who've asked you out and been turned down three times prior?"

A soft laugh flowed from her throat. "Actually there have. In fact, I've never went to lunch with a man from work in the seven years I've been here."

"So the county clerk is the steady lunch date you've had the whole three years I've been here?" He went on after she confirmed. "Is there a reason for this pattern of behavior?" Adam finally sat down in the seat behind him.

"There is." Eve tilted her chin with a smile. Her eyes unlocked with his for only a moment as she glanced over at the angel that just appeared behind him. She knew it was Adam's guardian, appointed by someone's strong prayers over him, but she was becoming curious as to who that was. "I'll have to tell you about it over lunch sometime."

Adam burst into laughter. "That's if I can ever convince you to have lunch with me. Otherwise I'll never know."

Seeing the opportunity to do some witnessing, Eve grabbed her purse and stood up to meet the challenge. "Convince me over lunch." When she glanced back to see if Adam was coming, she caught the look of surprise gleaming in his blue eyes, but he didn't hesitate in moving out of his seat. When she turned away where he couldn't see her face, her smile widened as a thought crossed her mind. *'If only he knew what he was in for.'*

Her endless witnessing could have been classified as a sermon. But she did manage to tell Adam why she wouldn't go to lunch with him or any other man she barely knew. Along with a sour prom date, she had thought Adam was older like all the other lawyers, another stereotype mistake. She hadn't known Tyler Jenkins well enough either, but she never expected he'd drive her anywhere but home. So when she found herself being tossed out of his car after the prom on a country road, she was devastated. All because she'd rejected his advances on her.

"Being blind had enough challenges of its own, then to add not knowing where you were on top of that…well, let's just say it turned my prom night into a nightmare. It was only with God's help that I finally found a house with two nice elderly people to help me." Eve went on to tell him how they called her mother and then let her wait in their home until Peggy showed up. After telling all that Eve insisted he talk for a while.

So Adam told her how he lost his wife and son three years ago in a tornado that went through Wichita. Which was what caused him to move back to Dodge City. He didn't give any details, and she didn't ask for any, since it was obvious it still bothered him.

She found out that the woman he had dinner with at the Brushfire restaurant was Helen Meade, the mother of a client he'd recently taken on. He told her how he was currently living in a garage apartment on his parent's ranch. He also mentioned that he'd like to build a house of his own someday. And that they had fifteen horses, and a hundred head of cattle.

"I've never seen that many cows." Eve's eyes gleamed just to imagine the sight.

"Then you'll have to come out sometime and see them. Maybe even learn how to ride a horse." His eyes danced back and forth as he admired the gleam in her apple green eyes.

"Now there's a challenge I don't think I could turn down."

"Then I'll be sure to let you know when I've got some free time." A gleam danced in his own eyes as he stood and held out a hand to help her to her feet.

Not knowing why his hand was proffered, she took it firmly and gave him a hardy handshake. Stating, "It's a deal."

Adam chuckled at her naïveté, and without releasing her hand when she attempted to withdraw it, he pulled her to her feet. The action was so unexpected that Eve nearly stumbled into his chest, since she was in motion on her own to stand as he pulled.

Being within inches of his face caused her to catch her breath and stagger backwards. She didn't breathe again until she was a comfortable distance from him. They both merely smiled, but made no comment.

When court re-adjourned Talbot was charged with vehicular manslaughter and sentenced to seventy years in jail with a possibility of parole after serving ten years.

Chapter 11

That Sunday Eve drove her mother and Lexi to church, since she'd passed her driving exam on Friday. Eve was a very confident driver, and her mother was a very nervous passenger. The fact that Eve had learned to drive in just one month was enough to make any caring mother a little nervous. Peggy should be used to it, since Eve learned everything easily, but this time there were other drivers out there to be worried about.

Eve was concerned about Mrs. Chadwick, since she wasn't in church. Thinking she must be sick, Eve asked Ryan about her, Chadwick's fifteen year-old grandson. "Is your grandma sick? Can I take her something for lunch?"

"Nah, grams is in the slammer. All she needs for lunch is a good lawyer." His tone was so nonchalant and sarcastic, that Eve actually stepped backwards because of it, which only seemed to amuse the boy more. "I know. I've got to be the only guy in town with a renegade granny." Ryan laughed as he walked off.

Eve was too shocked to ask him what she was in jail for. She knew there was no light in Irene Chadwick's eyes, but she never would have thought she was capable of committing a crime. She couldn't imagine her even Jay walking. After all, the lady was seventy years old, and one the nicest people in church. She was always helping others and doing nice things, or giving gifts to everyone, for every occasion.

Moments later Eve saw her mother talking to Ryan in the foyer. Then as the shock flushed Peggy's face, Eve knew she'd just heard the same horrible news. It turned into their whole topic of conversation during the short drive home. They were both skeptical and thought that Ryan might possibly be pulling a prank on everyone. But Eve would find out soon enough, as soon as Monday morning. Her mother wouldn't let her call the police station on a Sunday, or she'd find out sooner.

Eve no sooner finished washing and drying the dishes from lunch when Adam called to see if she was up to getting her first riding lesson. With nothing else to do on a beautiful Sunday afternoon, she couldn't find one reason to say no, so he said he'd be there to pick her up in fifteen minutes.

Eve dropped to dishtowel the moment she hung up and rushed off to change into a T-shirt and jeans.

She felt like a giddy schoolgirl, and she wasn't sure if it was the excitement of getting to ride, or the excitement of seeing Adam. He was very appealing to the eyes, and kind enough, but she couldn't let herself fall for a man that didn't share her love for God. And since Adam had no light in his eyes, she knew his love for God had grown cold. Hers on the other hand had been rekindled with the gift of her sight.

Eve was waiting on the front porch when he pulled up in a white Jeep. He had the top off the Jeep and a cowboy hat on. Eve hadn't seen him in a hat before, so the moment she climbed into the Jeep, she reached up to touch the brim of his hat.

The Bangora straw was stiff and course under her fingers. It brought a dance of delight to her eyes.

When Adam saw the joyous look on her face it sent a thrill up the back of his neck.

Eve let her hand fall away. "Why are you looking at me like that? I'm sorry if I've been too forward and offended you. I've just never seen you wear a hat before. Plus touching is an old habit of mine from being blind for thirty years. That used to be the only way I could see things."

"I understand and it's not that. I've just never seen so much delight in your eyes before." He put the Jeep into gear and pulled away from the curb. "Buckle up, please."

Eve was glad she'd pulled her long hair back into a ponytail once they got up to speed. Otherwise she'd be eating too much hair to respond. "I guess my eyes have never been so delighted before. I always relied on my other senses before." She fastened her seatbelt and turned to look over at him. "Did you know that the tip of your finger can detect a bump as small as 1/25,000 of an inch in height?"

Adam flashed a sideward grin. "No I didn't."

Eve nodded to reconfirm. "I was around two when I first discovered that. I found this mole on my cheek." She rubbed an index finger over the mole under her left eye. It made her giggle when she remembered what she had first thought it was.

"And why is that so funny?" The red light stopped them and gave him time to admire another delighted look wash over her face.

"Because of what I thought it was." She giggled again. "You see, I didn't know what a mole was even after mom explained it to me." Her mind quickly came up with another subject before she embarrassed herself by telling him she'd thought it was a booger, and then a bug. "My mom tried to help me understand colors by relating them to a smell. For example she told me that my hair was the color of cinnamon, then she had me smell the cinnamon. She said my eyes were the color of Granny Smith apples, so along with my hair she said I had all the sweet warm ingredients of a hot apple pie."

More like a cutie pie, Adam thought. He was afraid to glance at her and give away his thoughts, plus he didn't want to miss the turn that was just up ahead.

After driving through South Dodge, Adam turned on highway 56, and drove another mile or so before turning into a driveway. The arch above the cattle guard gate had the words Eden's Ranch burnt into the wooden plaque. Eve flashed an amused look at Adam when she read the sign.

"I know." Adam raised a hand in his defense. "The thought has amused me a few times too, especially since I grew up here with the name Adam, and now I've brought home a girl named Eve. But believe me, your name had no influence on me bringing you here." A soft chuckle escaped his throat. "I imagine dad will have a comment or two about it though, so maybe we can avoid both my parents for now. If I would have thought about you reading it, I'd have warned you ahead of time, but I didn't know..."

"My Aunt has been teaching me to read and drive." She explained quickly, pushing back the loose wisps of hair. "Your last name is Webber, so where did the name of the ranch come from? Is it that much of a paradise here?"

"No," Another soft chuckle curled his lips, "that was my mother's maiden name. This used to be my grandfather's place. In fact, he built it. The garage apartment I live in was originally built for his hired hand, which is where my dad started out when he first came here to work for my grandfather. Which is how him and mom met. He never left the place once he was here, he just moved into the main house after they married."

There was a huge pond to the right of the drive, with just enough trees around it to make it look like a garden to her. Clusters of cedar trees covered with some type of tiny blue berries caught her eye. Along with a couple of apple trees with their branches hanging low from the weight of the fruit.

Just when she thought the driveway would never end, she finally caught sight of a large house nestled in a clump of trees. It was a brown stone with arch-shaped windows and arch-shaped wooden shutters. It was a picture of perfection nestled in the trees with a view of the pond behind it.

On the other side of the drive there were two more buildings. One was a large newer Morton building. The other was an older garage type with the double-pitched roof, and double garage doors below, with a set of French doors to a balcony above. The garage was made from the same brown stone as the house, right down to the arch over the doors.

While they were riding Adam informed her how his grandfather had built both, the house and garage, from limestone he dug up from his own land. The garage used to be his grandfather's workshop. Stone cutting and carving was how he made extra money, when he wasn't too busy with ranch work or the oilrigs that were scattered over their property.

They didn't ride far from the house since Eve needed to get used to the sorrel gelding Adam had saddled for her. He said the horse's name was Lightning, since the jagged blaze on his face looked like a lightning bolt. The gelding Adam rode was named Buckshot, and he told her the color was called a flea-bitten gray, but as far as Eve could see it was a white horse covered with reddish-brown freckles.

"It's ironic that you should put me on a horse named Lightning, when it was lightning God used to give me my sight." She told him the story as it was told to her. Taking every opportunity she could to witness to him.

Although he already knew some of the story, since it was in the newspaper, but of course her version was more detailed.

Adam taught her the basics before mounting, then showed her again after he was on his horse. They rode for an hour that day, an hour and a half on Monday, and two hours on Tuesday. By Wednesday Eve was feeling pretty confident, especially after Adam told her she had great 'horse sense'.

She felt ready for another challenge, a race down the river trail sounded good to her, so before Adam was on his horse she took off shouting. "Last one to the river crossing is a rotten egg." She kicked the sorrel horse into a full-blown canter. Quickly discovering the horse had a lot of steam for his small size.

"Hey. Wait up." Adam shouted back as he hurried to get his saddle tightened. "What does she think she's doing? Why didn't I tell her he runs as fast as lightning too?" He mumbled to the only one listening, his horse.

Eve giggled, thinking how Adam was going to be the rotten egg. Her horse had run the whole mile and she still didn't hear Adam's horse coming behind them.

She reached the cluster of trees that marked the river crossing, and just as she turned her horse to cross the river, something large and green came down out of the tree in front of her. Lightning dug his heels into the ground to stop, then spun around so quickly that Eve lost her balance and fell off. The next instant her horse was running back the other way, and she was sitting on the ground looking up at the unshaved man towering over her in camouflaged gear from head to toe.

A repugnant smell of burnt sulfur filled her nostrils. Then terror swept over her when the dark spirit suddenly appeared behind the man. The very same spirit that had stolen the girl's soul from her body at the hospital, and once again the spirit hissed and showed his jagged teeth to see if she could still see him.

Suddenly Hamuel dropped down in the middle of everything with his sword drawn and wings spread – battled ready. With the rush of his swift entrance came a sweet rain garden scent that over powered the smell of burnt sulfur.

Chapter 12

A knock on the door brought Peggy out of her thoughts. When she opened the door, she was greeted by her sister's smile. "Come on in Maggy. What brings you in town this evening?"

"I came in for the Wednesday night service at your church that you asked me to come to. But low and behold, neither you or Evelyn were there, so I thought I'd stop by to find out if everything was okay." Maggy finally took a breath, then followed Peggy into the living room. She sat in the blue armchair next to Peggy's matching rocker. "So is Eve in her room sick?"

Peggy shook her head and let out a heavy sigh. "No, she's with that lawyer again. She's been out to his ranch everyday since Sunday to go riding with him. I'm hoping it's just a newly found passion for horses that she's discovered and not..." She moved her rocker into high gear as she suppressed her thoughts. "Oh well, never mind that. How was the service? I've had so much on my mind that I plum forgot about the guest speaker that was going to be there."

Maggy could tell from Peggy's vigorous rocking, that she did indeed, have a heavy load on her mind. "What lawyer are you talking about?" It also sounded like there was a tone of disapproval in her sister's voice.

"Adam Webber."

"Well..." Maggy raised a brow. "He is a very nice man, a handsome one too." Maggy suddenly let out an unexpected bout of laughter. "Is that why you're upset, because their names go together like bread and butter, or is it simply the fact that they're together?"

Peggy racked both hands through her short gray hair. From the frustration in her eyes it was obvious that was a question she was still trying to figure out herself. "Oh it's everything that's happened to her since she got her sight. She claims to see things, and I'm just finding that too hard to accept. I just wish she could see the heart break this growing relationship will lead her to."

"And what makes you so sure he's going to break her heart? I happen to know that his parents raised him in a good church with strong Biblical beliefs."

"I see the sparkle he puts in her eyes and I know how her other relationships have turned out. Even with that boy from our church that she dated."

Maggy smiled and pushed her, *Dutch Boy* cut, auburn dyed hair behind both ears. "You know you can't compare people like that. Besides they are both a lot more grown up than she was when she dated before, plus she's not blind anymore."

Peggy scoffed. "Love is blind, haven't you heard that one by now?"

"Oh come on Peggy. You're worrying yourself sick for nothing. Trust in her judgement. Trust in God."

"That's hard to do when I'm questioning her truthfulness these days."

"Will you just listen to yourself. Eve was never a liar, we both know that, so why would she be one now?"

"Because she claims to see angels and demons." Peggy slapped the arms of her chair out of her growing frustration.

"Then you better believe she can. Elisha and Daniel saw angels on several occasions." Maggy got up and walked across the room to the Bible on the desk. "If the finger of God came down in a bolt of lightning and touched you, do you think you'd remain the same? You should be sitting here thanking God for giving Eve her sight. But instead, you're sitting here wallowing in self-pity. Over what, your daughter's happiness? Psalms talks about the voice of the Lord striking with flashes of lightning, so the Lord could have spoken to Eve's eyes and told them to see *everything* clearly, and pow," Maggy slapped her hand down on top of the Bible to emphasize, "it was done." Then she sat back down to look up some scriptures for her sister to read.

Shock filled Peggy's eyes. "Do you really think I'm upset because she's happy?"

When Maggy nodded Peggy's head fell into her hands and she sobbed, asking God to forgive her. She had started out with simple concern and she had dwelled on it until it grew into a heavy mountain of worry. She had been feeling sorry for herself, because she felt like she was losing her daughter to Adam, and to the world.

Unseen

George Dixon still sat at his desk in his corner office of the police station. He should have gone home two hours ago, but he just couldn't tear himself away from the report in front of him. The Bixbee murder investigation was dragging out far too long. Here it had been five weeks into the investigation and no one from the forensic unit had even been out to go over the crime scene – which had been disturbed and grown cold in those five weeks. Dixon had dusted for fingerprints and collected all the evidence he could, but he didn't have the training necessary for a thorough sweep of the crime scene.

George Dixon was a tall thin black man who had grown up in Dodge City. He'd been on the force for seventeen years, since he was twenty, and he'd only been a detective for three of those years. He'd only seen three other murder cases that entire time. So George was still feeling very much like a novice at the whole thing. Especially when he had only been the detective on one of those other murder investigations.

Paco had been released from jail after just 48 hours, since they didn't have any substantial evidence to continue holding him. But Rachel was still in jail, since her fingerprints were all over the determined murder weapon. The lab had called to verify that much on the case, along with a few other tid-bits, like what the white fibers were and the fact that no blood or gun residue had been found on Rachel's clothing. Which could have simply meant that she might have had time to wash her hands or hide evidence. No discharged shell casing had been found at the scene, so Dixon was still hoping it'd turn up somewhere.

The phone rang and broke the heavy silence in the room. George picked it up, "Dixon here."

"Babe, when are you coming home? I've been holding dinner for an hour now." Katrina's voice was soft and soothing in his ear.

"I'm sorry Kat. I'm leaving right now, okay?"

"I'll see you in ten minutes then."

"Give or take a few." He checked his watch to make a mental note of the time.

"I'll take a few." She giggled, than added, "Love you Babe."

"Love you too." He smiled against the receiver. He couldn't believe he'd sat there absorbed in his thoughts for nearly three hours after his shift ended. There was just something about this case that didn't measure up. What was the girl's motive? Before he could get out of his chair, the phone rang again. This time it was Adam Webber calling back.

"I was just checking to see if you'd ever had a chance to talk to those EMS workers that were on duty the night Bixbee was taken to the hospital?" Adam questioned into the receiver.

"Yes I did, and I meant to get back with you on that, I'm sorry I've just been so busy." Dixon apologized. "Justin was the paramedic who treated her and he said she mumbled something about a child. But since there was no child involved that he was aware of, so he guessed she was delirious with pain or he hadn't heard correctly." After Adam thanked him and hung up, George hurried out of his office before his phone rang again.

Chapter 13

Adam spun his horse around when Eve's horse ran past him, he was about to chase it down, until a gut feeling brought on a sense of danger. Then he quickly spun his horse on its haunches and bolted in the direction Eve's horse had come from. He could only hope she wasn't hurt too badly.

With both hands at her side, Eve pushed herself up into a sitting position, but her eyes were still focused on the dark spirit as he reached down towards her. The man made the exact same gesture, at the exact same time, proffering a helping hand. Only Eve didn't see the help, so she scooted backwards on her hands and heels – like a schoolgirl playing crab soccer.

Hamuel raised his sword with both hands and was ready to strike downward when the dark spirit suddenly whirled his sword upward. The two swords crashed together with a thunderous clash and sparks spewed from the impact.

The man withdrew his hand quickly as if the sparks had singed him, but Eve continued to scoot backwards a few more feet. What finally stopped her from moving was when the dark spirit spoke to Hamuel.

"You're always getting in my way." The dark spirit hissed.

"And you always were a trouble maker Rage." Hamuel replied back.

The two spirits moved like the blink of an eye. Within seconds the battle was raging high above the tree the man had dropped from. Swords whirling and crashing together fiercely.

"I'm just trying to help you up. I'm not going to bite you." The man smiled and showed the slight gap between his top front teeth.

Her eyes left the battle scene for a moment to look at the man, noticing his gun for the first time since he'd been standing over her. Eve's pulse raced harder and pumped the lump in her throat bigger with each beat. She tried to swallow it back to respond, but it wouldn't budge. His dark unshaved jaw line made him look like a rogue soldier, because of the camouflage clothing he was wearing.

Her eyes averted back to the battle as Hamuel made contact with the dark spirits' shoulder. The spirit hissed in agony and fought back ever harder, but each of Hamuel's blows forced the demon backwards, further away from the protected one – Eve.

The man curiously followed her gaze, but all he could see was three tiny dots, which were his quails escaping into the distant sky. The sound of hooves diverted his attention to the approaching rider.

"What happened?" Adam asked as he swung down from his horse. He saw the frightened look on Eve's face and Bret standing over her holding a rifle. Suddenly Rachel's words raced through his mind. *I'd be more apt to think it was Bret...he's quick tempered.* "What happened?" He asked again in a louder tone of voice. His eyes were narrowly fixed on Bret as he helped Eve to her feet.

Bret offered another big smile that revealed his gapped teeth once more, followed by a devious laugh. "Settle down neighbor. I was just sittin' up in that tree about to nail me one from that covey of quail, when your friend comes runnin' up and scares 'em all off, so I dropped out of the tree to tell her to slow down."

A scowl creased Adam's otherwise smooth brow. "You know better then to jump out of a tree in front of a horse Bret. Especially one that's running." Adam shook his head with disgust. "You have horses at your place, you know better…"

Bret shoved his free hand deep into his pants pocket. "Sorry Miss. I didn't mean to make you fall. I figured if you were ridin' like that, you knew how to ride. I never figured you'd get throwed. I don't know what scared her so bad, but it wasn't me, cause she was lookin' at something over my head nearly the whole time." He motioned behind him by pointing in the general direction with the barrel of his rifle.

For the first time Eve noticed Bret's slight lisp, now that her pulse was settling down to normal. What was she going to say if Adam asked her what she was looking at? How could she tell him about the spiritual battle she witnessed? She glanced up to see if the battle was still going on. It looked like the dark spirit was fleeing, and Hamuel wasn't pursuing.

"Stop wheeling that gun around would yah. Quail season doesn't even open 'til November, so all you should be hunting is rabbit, especially since you're on our property. I realize dad gave you permission to hunt here, but not out of season." Without waiting for a comment from Bret, Adam turned his attention to Eve. "Are you okay?"

"I think so." She brushed the dust from her jeans feeling some soreness in her left wrist. "A few bruises to body and dignity, but other than that I'm okay."

"Again, I'm sorry Miss...ah...what's your name?" Bret turned an ear towards them so he wouldn't miss hearing her name. He'd never seen her before, so he gathered Adam had himself a new little girlfriend, something else he hadn't seen since Adam moved back to town.

"Evelyn..." Adam started until Eve interrupted.

"Eve, everyone calls me Eve." She jumped in mainly because she didn't want Adam to mention her last name. Knowing about the evil spirit that lurked around this man put Eve on the defensive side.

Bret let out another wicked laugh. "Really? Now that's funny, Adam and Eve, riddin' through the fields of Eden." He belted out another devious laugh. "What's the chances of that?"

"So you have heard something from the Bible." Adam led Eve over to his horse. They'd have to ride back together, since her horse was more than likely waiting for them at the barn.

"Very little." The smile finally left Bret's face.

Eve sensed that Bret didn't want to hear anymore conversation about the Bible. In fact, the moment Eve was mounted, Bret was walking off and saying good-bye. It was obvious that he not only needed to know more about the Bible, but about hunting out of season.

"If you move your foot out of the stirrup, it'll be easier for me to get up behind you." Adam smiled up at her.

"Oh...okay." She moved her foot, not realizing that they would have to ride back together, but then again, she hadn't been thinking about that anyway. It felt a little odd at first to have him so close to her. Close enough to feel the warmth of him on her back. "Ah...are you going to take the reins, or should I?"

"I can if you don't mind my arms around you." He smiled at the back of her head, knowing she couldn't see him. It was an appealing thought to him, but something told him that she wouldn't like the idea. His smile deepened when she simply took up the reins without commenting. His eyes closed briefly when the vanilla scent of her shampoo permeated his breath. *'Even her hair is sweet.'*

They were both silent for a long while, then Adam began to wonder what Bret was talking about, what had Eve been looking at? So he asked, but she avoided answering by telling him that she'd have to tell him over lunch someday. Silence fell over them the rest of the way back to the barn, and most of the way back to Eve's house, at which point Adam apologized for the rough evening she'd had.

"It's not your fault at all. It's actually mine for seeking a new challenge a little too soon. I have a tendency to deny my own limitations. I should have known I wasn't ready to race you yet." She assured him as she got out of his jeep. "I'll see you tomorrow."

"Sure." Adam nodded. Flashing a weary smile, he waved good-bye and backed out of the drive.

Once Eve was alone in her bedroom she prayed for understanding. It was then that Hamuel was instructed to tell her what she needed to know. Hamuel told her that the dark spirit's name was Rage and how he was usually with another dark spirit named Jealousy, obviously named after their main characteristics. Hamuel also told her that she had done well by praying first for understanding, that showed she was looking to God first, not angels.

Chapter 14

The next morning Bret sat down at the breakfast table ready to tell his father about the incident at Eden's ranch. It had been late yesterday when his dad got home, so he didn't get to talk to him.

Herb glanced up from his newspaper as Bret sat down at the other end of the table. "How many times do I have to tell you not to wear your hat at the table?"

Bret's shoulders slumped slightly at his father's roughness. But he promptly removed the ball cap from his head. "I saw Adam yesterday." He let out one of his devious chuckles. "And guess what. He was with a girl named Eve. Adam and Eve, what are the chances of that?"

"I guess that's his business who he dates." Herb lowered his nose back in the newspaper; more interested in it than anything Bret had to say.

The dark spirit named Jealousy suddenly appeared over Bret's shoulder and whispered into his ear. *"He's more interested in the paper than he is you."*

A crease formed over Bret's brow as he poured himself a cup of coffee. "I don't care who he dates. I just thought it was funny that he's dating someone named Eve and that they were at Eden's ranch together."

Herb lowered his paper once more to look over the top at Bret, with a crease forming in his own brow. "Is that where you saw them?" He went on after Bret nodded and shoveled a scoop of eggs onto his plate. "What were you doing over there?"

"Huntin' quail."

Rage was instantly behind Herb squeezing Herb's head between both of his wiry hands.

"Quail!" Herb shouted. "I hope you didn't tell Adam that. If you'd use your pea brain you'd remember he's a lawyer *and* a hunter. He knows quail season isn't open 'til November. Do you want them to turn you in or forbid us to hunt on their land? I've told you before, if you're going to hunt out of season, do it on our land, not theirs."

"Well they gave us permission…"

"They gave us permission to hunt in season and they can revoke that privilege at any time!" Herb folded his newspaper and slammed it on the table.

Rage squeezed his head even harder until Herb's face turned red.

Lolita came out of the kitchen with a plate of bacon, but she stopped in her tracks when Herb slammed down the paper. Herb saw her and motioned for her to bring in the plate. As his cook and housekeeper, Lolita had seen and heard a lot of things over the ten years she has worked for them, and she saw several reasons why his wife, Bailey, had left him.

Herb was very jealous, overly possessive, a perfectionist, arrogant and openly macho. Yet at the same time, he was so insecure that he wouldn't let Bailey leave the ranch very often without him. In fact, when Lolita had helped Bailey pack the day after their divorce, Bailey had used the words; *"He consumes me."*

Lolita sat the plate down on the table, then asked in her heavy Spanish accent, "Is there anything else I can get for you señor Louis?"

"Some hot coffee." Bret answered from the other end of the table and held the pot out to her. From the anger in his voice it was obvious that he was still bothered by his father's disapproval, which was now trickling down on her. "This stuff is cold."

Rage was now tormenting Bret right along with Jealousy.

Lolita looked at Herb for his nod of confirmation before she took the pot into the kitchen to refill it. She could almost feel sorry for Bret, if he wasn't so rude and immature about everything. It was obvious to her that Bret carried around a huge chip on his shoulder, because he rarely got his father's approval and he wasn't the favorite son. Bret's older brother Harley had been the favorite son, until he sided with Bailey and left with her.

Lolita and her older brother Paco not only worked on the ranch, but they both lived in a trailer next to the trailer Rachel and Lisa lived in. She had gotten Paco a job there within her first year, since she was only nineteen at the time, and she felt very uncomfortable being there alone with two men. It wasn't until three years later when Rachel came to work for them, then just two years ago Lisa had come to work there.

Rage was once again tormenting Herb's thoughts.

When Lolita returned with the coffee, she overheard Herb scolding Bret for his negligence on Eden's ranch. Herb was pumping Bret for the rest of the story and getting angrier with every breath. Especially when he found out that Eve had been thrown from her horse in the incident. It caused such a thick tension in the air, that Lolita was glad to get back into the kitchen to get away from it.

Adam couldn't believe the next case he was about to embark on – a shoplifter who was seventy-two years old. Adam found himself with more clients now than when he was in Wichita, and even with his fees somewhat lower, he was making more money because of the client ratio.

Irene Chadwick sat very upright across the table from Adam. Her hands properly folded on the tabletop. Her blue-gray bouffant hair was nearly flattened to her head from the week spent in jail without hairspray. She had such a polished mannerism that it was very hard to think of her being accused of shoplifting, or any offense for that matter. He had tried to get one of the other attorneys from his small firm to take the case, but they were even busier than he was.

"So Mrs. Chadwick, I hear they have you in here on shoplifting charges. Is there any truth to these accusations?" Adam clicked out his ballpoint pen with his thumb and readied a tablet in front of him while he waited on her answer.

"Yes, I've taken things from Raymond's Department store for twenty years." She shifted in her chair and lifted her chin with dignity. Not the least bit ashamed of her actions. "Why...those tyrant Raymond brothers," She blew out a breath in disgust. "They are so outrageous on all their prices and they're getting filthy rich at the expense of others. So I've been playing the modern day Robin Hood, if you will, taking from the rich and giving to the poor and less fortunate."

Oh Boy! Sounds more like a modern day nut case. Adam blew out his own exasperated breath as a dozen thoughts raced through his mind. Pushing his personal thoughts aside, he advised her, "You're not going to want to word it that way when we get in the courtroom, or they'll want you evaluated by a psychiatrist."

"Then let 'em. They'll find I'm very sound-minded, and not one bit forgetful. Why, I haven't forgot a single birthday or anniversary of one church member in twenty years." Again she lifted her chin with pride at her memory.

Adam dropped his forehead into his hand then squeezed the bridge of his nose between his thumb and forefinger. This wasn't going to be an easy case like he first thought it might be. After nearly an hour of deliberation they were finally able to come up with something they agreed upon. But Adam still left there with a headache, so he was glad that he didn't have to be in court with her until the following morning at nine A.M.

He wasn't sure which was more shocking to him, the fact that she went to church and didn't see anything wrong with stealing, or the fact that she had been doing it for twenty years. He had even asked her if her church taught the Ten Commandments, she said yes, but she still didn't think what she was doing was stealing, since she gave away everything she took.

Detective Dixon was just about to leave the police station to have lunch with Adam, when the phone stopped him. It was Ashley from the forensics lab in Great Bend. She was calling to let him know that a crime scene investigator was finally coming to work the Southwind murder case.

Chapter 15

Eve's heart sank when she saw Mrs. Chadwick walk in the courtroom with Adam. She had hoped she wouldn't be the one transcribing her trial. The one thing that added a ray of hope, besides the fact that she had one of the best attorney's in Dodge, was when she saw Irene's angel drift in behind her. There was still no light in Irene's eyes and no remorse there either, but at least there were some strong prayers going up on her behalf.

The bailiff, Matt Masters, declared that all should rise as judge Knapp entered the room.

Then the clerk stated the case, "Edgar and Eugene Raymond v. Mrs. Irene Chadwick on charges of shoplifting and petty theft. Case number…" Venus glanced over at Eve, then read off the case and docket numbers, she knew the woman was a member of Eve's church.

Eve caught her glance, and lowered her head in shame; as if she should be ashamed of someone else's crime, but it did leave a dark reflection upon her church that she disliked.

Once Venus was seated, Victor Dillon rose and walked around in front of his table in his usual manor.

Victor had been the Raymond's attorney for nearly fifty years. In fact, he has defended the whole Raymond clan at one point or another, and there was an even dozen just counting the children in their two families. Edgar and his brother Eugene were in their mid-eighties. They both should have long since retired, but neither one of them could seem to let go and turn things over to any of their sons. So they both still ran the store themselves, with one son each helping manage it.

"My clients have suspected Mrs. Chadwick of shoplifting on numerous occasions, they've just never been able to prove anything before. This time they have videotape evidence to offer the court. I'll enter this as exhibit A." Dillon approached the bench with the tape and laid it down in front of judge

Knapp. "They've had video surveillance for two years now, and were finally able to catch Mrs. Chadwick red handed on August 1st of this year."

Knapp handed the video off to the bailiff. "Will you run this video for the court to see?"

Matt pushed the tape into a VCR that had been brought into the room earlier that morning. The tape was played. It left no doubt that it was Mrs. Chadwick dropping a watch into her handbag. After doing so, she glanced around to make sure no one had seen her, which indicated that she knew what she'd done was wrong.

"Do you have anything further to add Mr. Dillon?" The judge inquired before turning her attention to the defendant, once Dillon shook his head and resumed his seat. "Mr. Webber, what does your client have to say about these charges and this evidence against her?"

Adam cleared his throat as he stood to address the judge. "Your honor, my client pleads guilty, and due to her age she asks that the court grant her community service. She would also like to do volunteer work at Raymond's department store until they render her debt paid in full. If that is acceptable with the plaintiffs and this court."

Before the judge could even ask Dillon and his clients, they all had their heads together in deep discussion over the plea. "Well, gentlemen?" Diane

Knapp finally questioned after giving them a few moments to discuss.

The brother's were in disagreement, but Dillon quickly managed a compromise. "My clients would like a cash settlement of one hundred dollars, all court costs paid, and for one full year of volunteer labor from the defendant, besides her community service."

Judge Knapp pressed her hands together, as if she was praying, rolling things over in her head. "Since there's no real proof of any other stolen items, and the watch only has retail value of fifty dollars, that's all they'll get for a cash settlement. The defendant will be liable for all court costs. Considering the defendant's age and admittance of guilt, her volunteer labor shall not exceed six months. Likewise for the community service." Diane finalized her judgement.

After a few other small cases court recessed for lunch.

It was becoming more often that Adam joined Eve and Venus for lunch. There had only been a few times, since Eve accepted his first invitation, that he hadn't joined them. Only because he had to met with a client.

This time when he told Eve he had to meet with a client, he added an offer for dinner and horseback riding later in the day.

She informed him that she was suppose to have dinner at her Aunt's with her mom. Then before giving it much thought she invited Adam to go to Maggy's with them. When Adam agreed, she went on to meet Venus for lunch.

"Where's your new sidekick?" Venus had teased when Eve showed up at their usual restaurant without Adam.

Eve explained that he was merely a friend, but she was beginning to wonder what Adam thought they were. If he thought they were a couple, he hadn't said. But when she thought back on it, she had seen him nearly everyday since their first ride together, if not at work, after work or over lunch or dinner.

"He'll be going over to Aunt Maggy's with me later for dinner." Eve's brows drew together at Venus' expression. "And just what is that look suppose to mean? You know I'm still not good at reading peoples facial expressions."

"It means...this guy is becoming a *bigger* part of your life than you realize." Venus mopped up some catsup with her French fry. "Face it girl, he's with you everyday at lunch, then again after work most nights. Now you're taking him to meet your family."

"He's been teaching me how to ride horses, that's all, and we're becoming friends in the process. Besides, he's already met my family, he went to school with Troy and he knows my Aunt Maggy from the courthouse, so I'm not *taking* him to meet my family"

"Okay, keep telling yourself that." Venus raised a hand to free herself from any further discussion on the matter. "So what's the deal with this Mrs. Chadwick? Doesn't she go to your church?"

Eve nodded and said she didn't want to discuss it beyond that. She didn't want to slip and mention the fact that she hadn't seen the light in Irene's eyes. Since the hospital Eve hadn't said anything else to anyone, except to her Aunt, about being able to see into the spiritual realm. If her own family hadn't believed her, how could anyone else? She had wanted to tell Adam about it several times, but she hadn't, she didn't want him to think she had lost her mind.

Peggy was upset with Eve when she found out that Adam was going to have dinner with them. Eve assured her that she had called Maggy from work to make sure it was okay, and Maggy didn't have a problem with it, so she couldn't understand why her mother would.

After stating her feelings on the matter, Peggy remained quiet while they waited for Adam to come and pick them up. Peggy had said that it was supposed to be a family dinner and that Adam was not part of the family. And she silently hoped Adam wouldn't become family. She had tried to have a better attitude since talking with Maggy about him, yet she still couldn't help but think that Eve could do better.

When Adam arrived he wasn't driving his jeep as usual. Instead he had borrowed his mothers Sable to drive them in, stating how he wanted Peggy to be more comfortable in a nicer car. Which stabbed at Peggy's guilty conscience and made her feel the harsh sting of her quick judgment, yet it wasn't enough to make her admit she may have been wrong.

Adam's charm and appeal went over well with Aunt Maggy and Uncle Alex. Adam and Alex talked a lot about golf and dogs, which were two of Alex's favorite subjects, besides his woodworking. Which after dinner, Alex took Adam out to show him his workshop, and his latest wood project.

Eve suspected that Alex showed him the dogs while they were out there too. Dixie was a golden Labrador, and the mother of Eve's dog. Dan was a black Labrador, and the brother to Eve's dog. So both dogs had been a big part of the family for the past ten to twelve years. Alex was sure to do some bragging on them, especially since he and Maggy never had any children of their own to brag on.

"You've been awful quiet tonight Eve. Is something wrong?" Maggy asked as they finished cleaning in the kitchen and moved into the living room.

"I guess I've just been thinking about Mrs. Chadwick. I had to transcribe her trial today, and there wasn't the least bit of remorse in the woman's face at all."

"She could be loosing her mind and..." Maggy tried to excuse.

"No." Eve interrupted. Shaking her head in disagreement. "I think she's just hardened her heart and doesn't see the wrong anymore."

"Eve." Peggy scolded with a firm tone. "That's not your place to judge that. The woman has done so many nice things for so many people. Why...it's been such a shock to the entire church that this even happened. You can't see what's in a persons' heart, no matter how much you think you can see into things..." Peggy cut herself off before saying something too harsh that she couldn't take back.

"No mother, it's because I didn't see the light in Mrs. Chadwick's eyes, so I know..." Eve stopped herself just as Adam and Alex walked through the front door. She knew that they had heard enough to know whom she was talking about, but she didn't want to carry the conversation any further. Since she didn't want to have to explain things to Adam. Normally it didn't matter to her what people thought of her, but for some reason it did matter what Adam thought of her, she just wasn't sure why.

Peggy seemed more talkative on the way home, as if she were feeling more comfortable with Adam. Maybe even deciding that she liked him and had been too quick in judging him. Of course Eve knew she'd never admit to anything.

"I'd like to talk to you for a moment." Adam stopped Eve before she got too far away from the car.

"I'll be there in a minute mom." Eve called to her mother and motioned for her to go on in the house. "What is it?" She asked as she turned her attention back to Adam.

"I hope you and your family weren't judging Mrs. Chadwick too harshly because of what she's done. She did think she was doing something good. Like being a modern day Robin Hood, is how she put it. She said that everything she stole was given away, that she kept nothing…"

"It's not like you're thinking Adam. We weren't judging her at all. Besides, it doesn't make it right to steal just because you give it away"

"I realize that. So then what did you mean by not seeing any light in her eyes?"

Eve's heart leaped. '*So he had heard that part,*' she thought. She glanced over to Hamuel in question, but he simply raised his hands letting her know it was completely her decision what she told him. The next instance, Hamuel was suddenly on the roof of her house, as if giving them some room to talk. "It's a long story and…"

"And…you're not going to do this again are you? Put me off until later, then later never comes. Like the day you got thrown because of Bret. Even if I wasn't a lawyer I'm not the kind of guy who just forgets things and lets them drop. It's time you started trusting me Eve." He reached out and pulled her by the hand to get her to sit back down in the car to talk to him. "Why can't you trust me anyway? Have you been that hurt in the past that you'll never trust me?"

"Oh, it's not that at all. It's more like, will you believe me if I tell you. When I first told my own family they didn't want to believe me, so why should you?" Eve squirmed in her seat like a little girl getting scolded.

"Try me and see." Adam pleaded through gentle blue eyes.

Eve took a deep breath. "Okay, you asked for it…" Eve explained to him how she not only gained her physical sight, but her sight into the spiritual realm, and gave him some of the details of what she had seen, including the battle the day Bret had caused her to get thrown. She told Adam about his angel and Mrs. Chadwick's, even though there was no light in their eyes. Then she explained to him about the light and what it meant.

Adam was stunned, but wasn't sure what to say to dispute the issue with her. He knew he had drifted away from the Lord and let his light go out. "Okay, so what's my angel's name?" He hoped her answers would either convince him or at least give him a point he could dispute.

"Let me find out." Eve turned and asked the angel sitting on the hood of the car what his name was. "He said his name is Abijah." As Eve said the name, Hamuel was suddenly beside the car again.

Adam couldn't stop himself from chuckling at the sound of the name, since it sounded so made up. Doubt began to flood over his thoughts. "Okay, then ask him how long the ozone layer has had a hole in it."

Eve could hear both angels laughing before she turned to look at them. Her face lit up with a delighted smile as her gaze moved from Adam to the angels beside her.

"What's he saying?" Adam asked with deep interest. He was curious to know what had put such a pleasant look on her face. A look that clearly stated she was hearing something or someone, whether real or delusional was the next question.

"They're both laughing. Oh, I wish you could hear the sound of their laughter. It's such a sweet sound. It's a reverberating sound like they're laughing through water."

"I didn't think my question was funny?" He frowned.

Eve held up a finger to hush him so she could listen to what Hamuel was beginning to say.

"You people of the seeing world." Hamuel let out another soft laugh. "Fix your eyes not on what is seen, but on what is unseen for only that is eternal, then you might know such things. There has always been a hole in the ozone. It is only because of your growing technology that you are now able to *see* these things. It is the gateway to heaven, just as the Bermuda Triangle is the gateway to the abyss. The ozone hole is getting bigger because of all the rising chemicals, but it has been there since the creation of earth."

While Eve relayed the response to Adam the look of skepticism faded from his eyes. She could tell that the more she spoke, the more he believed what she was saying. It was a boost to her confidence that he believed her.

After she was finished Adam was silent for a moment. Then he started telling Eve how he used to go to church and how he knew his mother was still praying for his return. He knew that he needed to get back into church, but he just kept putting it off.

Eve knew it was time to go in the house when her mother flicked on the porch light, as if to signal to her. Eve apologized through her embarrassment and bid him goodnight.

Chapter 16

That night Eve fell asleep quickly, but awoke just as quickly in the middle of a terrifying dream. She bolted upright in bed and she saw something lurking outside her window. He appeared to be an angel, since he had the same luminous clothing like Hamuel wore, but it wasn't Hamuel. Plus his eyes were solid black, no color or light was present.

"Eve." He called to her. "Come here, Eve." The angel called again.

Eve tossed back the covers and went over by the window to see what he wanted. Peering through the mini blinds she spoke back to him. "What do you want?"

"Open the window and let me come in then I'll tell you what it is I want." He spoke in a low voice.

"Why can't you tell me now?" She frowned.

"There must be no barrier between us and the window is causing a barrier. Don't you see? Hurry, Lexi is in trouble and she needs your help." His tone was urgent.

Without another delay Eve put her hands on the window locks and was about to open it when Hamuel swooped down out of nowhere. His sudden appearance caused the other angel to back away from the window.

Hamuel's wings and sword were battle ready, which meant he sensed trouble. "Do not listen Eve. If he was a true angel of light he could enter without you letting him in."

The spirit threw a fiery dart through the window at her. When it made contact with her arm, fearful thoughts swept through her mind at the same instant, although she didn't feel the piercing sensation of the dart itself.

"Stop it." Eve cried out.

He threw another flaming dart before Hamuel attacked him and unmasked his true identity. The radiant white was suddenly transformed into a tarnished gray, revealing the dark spirit underneath.

Unseen

Hamuel raised his shield and blocked the next dart he attempted to throw at Eve. Then he swung his sword and the two spirits were soon dueling like two knights in heavy battle. Each blow of Hamuel's sword drove the dark spirit further away from Eve's window.

Eve prayed as she watched the battle rage on. With every word she spoke in prayer, she could see Hamuel's speed and strength increase, while the dark angel's power weakened. That encouraged her to pray even harder, and when her prayer increased the dark angel suddenly vanished like a puff of smoke.

Because she'd prayed for understanding, Hamuel was permitted to explain things to her. He told her that it was a dark angel named Fear that had come to attack her, because she had exposed the spirit realm to Adam, and they didn't like being exposed. He also told her that Rage was not the only dark spirit that knew she could see into their world. He told her how the Bible tells how Satan himself masquerades as an angel of light, and that she must always look for the light in their eyes, since that is the only way to see the truth in their heart. He also warned her again not to speak to them, because they would only try to deceive her, as this one had done using Lexi's name.

Unseen

Eve had spent the rest of her weekend fasting, praying and reading her Bible. She hadn't even stopped long enough to accept any phone calls, which Peggy seemed all too grateful to intercept for her, especially those from Adam.

Come Monday morning Eve felt rejuvenated and ready for another week. At least that's what she thought until a murder arrangement came before the court.

Rachel Meade couldn't have been more than mid to early twenties. So young and innocent looking. How could she possibly murder anyone? But then after Irene Chadwick, Eve had learned, looking innocent didn't necessarily prove innocence. The one difference was that Rachel had the light in her eyes, Eve caught the slightest glimpse of that from across the room.

What was even more disturbing was when Eve discovered who the murder victim was. It was the girl from ER who's spirit Eve had seen taken from her body. A picture of the girl – minus the blood – was presented to the court, and a name to go with it, Lisa Bixbee. Another pretty girl in her early twenties. Both girls worked at the same ranch, Southwind Quarter Horse Farm, Adam's neighboring ranch.

Images of Lisa's bloody body on a gurney, the dark spirit named Rage snatching her spirit away, and Bret's evil laughter flashed through Eve's mind like snap shots. The dark spirit was a definite link between the two; she just had to figure out where and how.

"My defendant pleads not guilty your honor, and requests a jury trial."

Adam's comment brought Eve out of her thoughts as she noted his comment into her stenograph.

"Very well. This case will be adjourned for two weeks. That should allow enough time to gather our jury members?" Knapp questioned before dismissing. Once Tracy Powers stood and confirmed, court was recessed for lunch.

Adam leaned over towards Rachel. "This will also give the guy from forensics time to investigate the case more thoroughly, since he just arrived Friday."

"I just hope he finds something to clear me." Rachel frowned and took a deep breath as the bailiff came to take her back to her cell.

The orange jumpsuit was about to engulf Rachel after being in jail for seven weeks. It was obvious that she hadn't been eating or sleeping well. Adam had tried to get her out on bail, but the bail had been set so high that neither her nor her mother could come up with it. Adam had nearly put up the bail himself, but he'd learned the hard way, not to get that involved with a client.

Over lunch Eve tried to get Adam to tell her what he knew about the case. Since Venus was unable to join them, Eve was able to speak freely; "I saw her angel and the light in your clients' eyes, so I have to doubt whether or not she committed this murder. Do you think she did it?"

"That's irrelevant. I *have* to believe my client when I agree to take a case, whether I truly believe them or not, it's my job to believe them. But if I have serious doubt, then I usually don't take on their case." Adam let out a sigh. He could clearly see that his answer wasn't enough to satisfy Eve's curiosity. "Okay, I think she was at the wrong place at the wrong time and made the biggest mistake anyone could possibly make, which is touching the murder weapon."

After their food arrived at the table, Adam went on to say how it hadn't helped anything that it took seven weeks for a crime scene investigator to show up. "What good does it do to scan over a cold crime scene? The real killer had enough time to cover his tracks three times over."

"Have hope. Something may turn up that was over looked before." Eve was her usual optimistic self.

"I don't know." Adam shrugged his broad shoulders. "There's been too much time for things to get moved and tromped over."

"So if she didn't do it. Who do you think did?"

"I don't know." He let out another heavy sigh. "Look, I really shouldn't say anything further on the case since it's still under some investigation, not to mention the lawyer- client confidentiality."

Eve let the subject drop from her lips, but it still weighed heavy on her mind. She couldn't help but think there was a reason she had witnessed the victim's spirit being torn from her body, along with the fact that she'd be transcribing the trial. Eve now knew that nothing happened by mistake or by chance, that there was a reason for everything. Could this possibly be her mission that Hamuel had spoken of?

Chapter 17

First Colby Daubs' baby sister Mandy is killed by a drunk driver, which was hard enough to fathom, little alone another murder occurring on the same night. Colby was only a twenty-year-old rookie on the police force, but they were still assigning him to work with detective Dixon on the Bixbee murder case. But he didn't dare complain to the chief about it, especially since he'd just asked Chief Harry Crow three weeks ago to keep him as busy as possible. Work had been the only way he could keep his sister's death from being the focal point of his thoughts. Colby believed in God, but it was hard to imagine God would let a thing like this happen.

"Come on Daubs."

Colby's olive green eyes looked up from the file on his desk. He saw Dixon looking at him from the doorway of his office. When their eyes met, Dixon nodded his head towards the exit.

"We've got to meet Woodrow at his hotel and take him to the crime scene."

Colby grabbed his hat off his desk, placed it over his light brown crew cut, and followed Dixon to the exit. He didn't know much about the case, since he'd just been told about his new assignment and given the file that morning. But he figured he was about to find out all he'd need to know, since they were going to be talking to the forensics expert and going over the crime scene with him.

"We should have had this done Friday. It's almost as if Herb and Bret Louis knew we were coming." Dixon went on as they climbed into his unmarked Chevy. "I don't know how they could have found out about Woodrow being here on Friday, but it was sure convenient for them to leave town and lock up the office. Who on earth would have a hired hand that isn't trusted enough to have his own key to a *barn* office? Especially when he's allowed in the house. Go figure."

"It's got a definite fishy smell to it." Colby managed to get a few words in.

"Rotten fish. I'm beginning to wonder if we're not fishing up the wrong stream."

"What?" Colby scowled in confusion. "We know the murder was committed there…"

"Not the wrong place. Wrong fish…*person*." Dixon corrected his young apprentice. "Their convenient absence just makes me wonder if they have something to hide. Why else would they stall us? I mean it's not like the crime scene isn't already as cold as bologna in a meat locker."

"Exactly. So if they were going to hide something, they could have done it way before now. Maybe they did have legitimate business out of town."

Dixon let out a huff. "I'm gonna find out if they did. You can hang your hat on that."

Todd Woodrow was waiting in front of the hotel's restaurant when Dixon pulled up. Once he recognized the black driver of the car as Dixon, he bent down, picked up his tool bag, and walked over to meet the car. He climbed into the back seat after a curt nod to both men in front. Todd had been with the Great Bend forensics lab for two years and he'd worked with Dixon a couple times before. Fortunately the other two cases turned out to be natural deaths instead of murder.

"I thought maybe you'd have those blond curls buzzed off by now." Dixon teased with a chuckle.

Todd racked a hand through his hair. "I did cut it pretty short after I left here the last time, but that's been over a year now, so it's grown back several times. At least it's not touching my collar yet." He smiled. His hair was a lot shorter on the top and sides than it was in the back.

Dixon had razzed him pretty hard the last time about his curly blond hair. Saying how Todd should go into the modeling business instead of police work. Dixon thought any officer of the law should wear his hair above the collar, if not a buzz cut. He'd also thought that an officer should set a good example to the public.

Dixon checked the seat beside him to make sure the warrant was still where he put it. Without it, they might not get back into the crime scene for another look, so he wasn't about to make the drive without it.

On the way to Southwind Dixon collaborated with Woodrow over the evidence. Daubs was able to get the details that he'd missed, like the fact that all ten of Rachel's fingerprints were found on the murder weapon, and that the blood on the bottom of her boot was a positive match with the victim's DNA. They also had an eyewitness who saw her coming from the direction of the crime scene with the murder weapon, as well as three others witnesses who seen her with the weapon moments later.

"The odd piece to this puzzle is the bite mark on the vic's neck that you told me about over the phone." Dixon shook his head still wondering how, or if, it fit into the crime.

"The bruising isn't post-mordum, so the lab estimates it happened within twelve to sixteen hours prior to her murder, so it didn't happen during the murder or as a result of it." Woodrow assured Dixon.

"So our vic may have just had an all around bad day from beginning to brutal end." Dixon added as the possibilities played through his mind. Yet there seemed to be a few small holes in the overall case. Like motive, what did the killer stand to gain?

Woodrow went on to say how the bite imprint was no match with the suspect, so therefore it didn't appear to be linked to the crime in anyway. Especially since the cause of death was a gunshot to the abdomen. There was also no apparent struggle and the crime was in no way a sexual assault.

Herb was all too eager to be of any help once they reached the ranch. He let them in the office and even answered all of Woodrow's questions about his whereabouts the night of the murder, etc. He maintained his story about being in bed, and said his son Bret could verify the fact. Then he left them to their business and went back up to the house.

As they stepped in the door Daubs made a quick scan of the room. To their right was an old oak desk with a small outside window behind it. Then the wall facing the door was lined with bookshelves, and to the left was a leather sofa that sat facing the desk, it matched the leather armchair that sat behind the desk. The room was approximately ten feet wide by twelve feet long, like all the stalls in the barn, since it was set up for breeding purposes.

Woodrow sprayed the floor with a solution from his kit bag. Then he turned out the light and shut the door to make the room as dark as possible. When he turned on the light from his kit, a large purple pool appeared on the floor, spatters and all. He followed the spatters with his light and sprayed a little more solution on the shelving. It verified what Dixon had told him about the victim facing the door with her back to the shelves. But it also told him where the shooter was standing, which was within very close range of the victim, close enough to be holding the gun directly to the vic. Only there was no gunpowder found on the vic.

"The white fiber found on the vic is consistent with the polyester fiber used to stuff most pillows. And since there was no powder residue on the vic, I'd have to say that the shooter used a pillow to muffle the shot. Holding the pillow to the Vic's body with the end of the barrel. Luckily the bullet lodged in a bone so we were able to recover it and match it to the weapon.'" Todd indicated the angle of trajectory as he faced the shelves and pictured the scene in his head. Then his eye caught sight of it. Opening a small envelope Todd used his tweezers to remove it from the bookshelf. Dropping it into the envelope he turned and said, "Looks like more fiber from our missing pillow."

"So what did the killer do with the pillow?" Dixon held up a hand towards the leather sofa. "No pillow was ever found."

"Obviously it was disposed of."

"Our suspect was seen leaving the scene with the gun, so she didn't have time to hide a pillow anywhere except in the barn. We did a thorough search and never found anything else." Dixon defended.

"You never found a shell casing either, but that didn't mean there wasn't a bullet fired." Todd raised a challenging brow towards Dixon.

Dixon's shoulders slumped forward. "Where could she have hid it with as little time as she must have had?" He stepped out the door and surveyed the breezeway of the barn intently. He tried hard to recall exactly what it looked like the night of the murder. He seemed to remember something large at the far end of the breezeway, but what? It had been dark then. All that was there now was a large doorway that stood open to let the sunlight stream in, same as the other end of the breezeway. He'd have to go back over the report and his notes to see if anything was mentioned there. Surely he had mentioned it somewhere, since he was such a stickler for details.

They talked to Paco and Bret before they left. Woodrow had wanted to talk to Paco's sister before he left, since she was the housekeeper. Only Lolita had gone after groceries, so it meant they would have to get her to come into the station later. And Dixon knew they would, since Woodrow was a lot like him, and would leave no stone unturned. Dixon had already talked with Lolita once, but Woodrow still wanted a word with her himself, just in case she remembered or noticed anything different since that night.

Chapter 18

Tuesday morning before heading to the courtroom, Eve went across the street to the police station to pay a visit to Rachel Meade. She felt a strong need to talk with the girl in person, in doing so, she hoped to gain an understanding why God had laid this girl upon her heart.

Eve went to the police chief first to see if she could even get in to see Rachel.

"If I didn't still owe you one for getting Jo Lynn a job at the hospital in medical records." Chief Harry Crow let out a heavy sigh, knowing it wasn't very ethical for Eve to be seeing a prisoner, at least not when she'd soon be transcribing her trial for state records. But he knew Eve well enough to know that she wouldn't add any off record information to the files. Yet he'd never known her to become so interested in a case before. He could only assume that perhaps she knew the girl personally, but he didn't ask.

"Thanks Harry." Eve stood up with a warm smile on her lips. "Now I owe you one, so if either of your two sons need jobs, send them my way."

Harry let out a hardy chuckle. "I'll do that, after I whip the feathers out of 'em."

Eve smiled at the endless humor he seemed to derive from his name. Harry's great-great-grandfather was a Native American Indian chief, and now that Harry was the chief of police, he had a lot of fun playing with that concept. Eve had once told him that he was as full of jokes as he was coffee, because she could always smell coffee on his breath. He'd become health conscious and got in shape after the mild heart attack he suffered six years ago, which is how Eve came to know him, since he was under her father's care at that time.

Eve knew both Shane and Trent had good jobs, so she figured that's why Harry would whip them if they lost them. Harry's wife, May Dawn, was the only one in the house not currently working. Harry said she'd been thinking about going back to work now that all their kids were grown and working.

Eve was nervous as she entered the visitation area to wait for Rachel. Her nerves were taking over, since she wasn't quite sure what she was going to say to Rachel, or where to begin.

"Can I talk to your angel for a minute?" Would not be a good start to their conversation, nor would, *"I saw your angel, so I know you're innocent...but can you tell me more?"* With her elbows on the table, Eve bowed her head into her clasped hands and prayed softly. Until all her thoughts faded into her prayer. *Lord, I need your help here, let me know what it is you'd have me say to her, and why it is you drew me in here today.*

Eve's heart skipped slightly when she heard the door open and the sound of footsteps heading towards her. She turned to see Rachel walking towards her with a puzzled look on her young face. Eve offered a warm thin smile as she stood and proffered a hand. "Hi, I'm Evelyn Kincaid."

"Rachel Meade...but then I guess you knew that, since you had to ask to see me." A scowl creased her smooth brow. "What exactly are you doing here? Are you a reporter after a story of something?"

"I'm a court reporter, but not like the kind that prints a story in the newspaper. I transcribe everything said in the courtroom for the county's records." Eve suggestively motioned towards the chair across from hers. "Please, can we sit and talk a minute? Or would you simply like me to pray with you standing up?"

Immediately the girl's face softened. "You came to pray with me?"

Eve offered a nod as she sat back down.

"Then God has heard my cries. I've been asking him to send a prayer warrior to me."

Eve couldn't be sure, but she thought she saw the light in Rachel's eyes intensify at the mere inkling that God was listening to her. "Of course God hears you. Why wouldn't he?" Eve had never considered herself a prayer warrior, and those were in no way the words she'd planned on saying to Rachel, yet they fell from her lips for a reason.

Rachel shook her head. "I don't know. I just didn't think he was listening anymore. I haven't been to church in so long, and I haven't even been able to read my Bible since I've been in jail."

"A lot of the disciples were put in jail, yet the Lord never stopped listening to their prayers. And I'll see if I can get them to give you a Bible." Eve made a note to herself so she wouldn't forget to do that. She tried hard to tune out Hamuel talking with Rachel's angel, but she couldn't tune it out completely.

"I know you're right, but none of them were accused of murder, where they?"

"No, but God knows you didn't murder anyone either, murder is not in your heart." Eve's words not only surprised her, but they brought tears to Rachel's eyes. Now Eve knew God was helping her with the words, since that was something else she hadn't planned to say. It was a reassurance to her that Rachel was indeed innocent.

"Oh...I wish you knew how good it makes me feel to know that someone else believes I'm innocent." Rachel reached across the table and took hold of Eve's hands. "God also knew I needed someone to pray with me." Her tears fell to the table as she bowed her head and waited for Eve to start praying.

As they prayed, Eve heard the angels become silent. She glanced up towards them and saw them both looking up and raising their hands to heaven.

The two women talked as long as the guard would allow them after they prayed. Rachel told Eve the same things she told Adam, so Eve was able to get the whole story, now she just needed to figure out what she was suppose to do with the information – if anything. Maybe God had simply drawn her there to pray with Rachel and offer her some encouragement.

Eve left knowing the girl was innocent, even before Hamuel told her that Rachel's watchman had told him the same story that she told Eve.

Chapter 19

After work Eve went by Adam's office to talk to him about her visit with Rachel, since she hadn't seen him all day.

Adam's secretary, Katrina or Kat as her husband would call her, said, "He's holding a will reading in another room. He'll be done in about thirty minutes if you want to wait." Katrina was married to detective George Dixon, a long time friend of Adam's, all the way from elementary school.

Eve agreed to wait, so Katrina let her in his office to wait. Eve sat in the chair in front of Adam's desk for a while. Then when she noticed some photo's on the desk she got up to take a peek, thinking it might be some family pictures or something. She was horrified when she discovered they were the coroner's photos of Lisa Bixbee. There was a photo of the bullet wound, along with one of an oval shaped bruise on the right side of her neck, and another of bruise marks on both shoulders. Eve noticed the coroner's report under the photos, so she scanned through it to find the cause of bruising.

"Grip bruising on shoulders from being restrained, and bite mark on neck with teeth impressions." Eve read the words aloud but still couldn't believe what they said. "Why would someone bite her neck? Or better yet, who?" Before she replaced the material back onto Adam's desk, she read that the report stated the bruising occurred hours prior to the shooting. With this new bit of information Eve paced the floor pondering on it.

She couldn't help but think there was some connection between the bruising and the murder, even though the report had ruled out a direct connection, since the events occurred hours apart. Yet Eve had to wonder if one event didn't lead into the other somehow.

Eve chewed her fingernails on one hand as she paced the floor in deep thought. She flinched when Adam entered the room, since she hadn't heard his footsteps approaching.

He smiled at her and walked around to take the seat at his desk. "Sorry, I didn't mean to startle you.

Normally you would have heard me walking down the hall before I ever made it to the door."

"Oh it's okay. I guess I was thinking too loud to hear you." She smiled back and finally sat back down.

"Since you're here, I guess that means you're accepting the invitation to dinner tonight with my parents and me?"

Eve searched her memory and did finally recall him asking her something about a dinner. "Oh, yeah. So I guess I came here for two reasons then."

"So what's the other reason?" He suddenly noticed the photos and paperwork on his desk. Scooping it all up, he tossed it into his briefcase and closed it.

"Ah…I already saw those. I'm sorry I even looked. Believe me." Eve laid a hand over her heart to express her sincerity. "I just thought they might be family photos or something and…"

A frown creased Adam's brow. "Next time, I'd appreciate it if you didn't look through things on my desk without asking first. Sometimes the photos from a case can be very ugly, like in the vehicular manslaughter case of Mandy Daubs. You don't need to see that kind of brutality. I don't even like seeing it, but it's necessary"

Eve's hand moved down to hold her stomach as she remembered the fact that Mandy had been nearly severed in half. Her stomach turned to think of what those photos might have looked like. "Oh I don't even want to imagine that." Pushing her hair back with her other hand, she adjusted her thoughts back to the reason she was there. "I talked to Rachel Meade today and I'm convinced of her innocence. Her guardian even confirmed it."

"Wait a minute." Adam raised a hand to stop her. "What are you doing talking to my client? And what do you mean by guardian? Like as in her guardian angel?"

"Yes her angel." She offered a nod before standing to resume her pacing. "I guess I just had to know what happened that night." She took a deep breath before going on. "The night all this happened was the night I came out of the coma. I had such a throbbing headache from all the new information my mind and eyes were taking in, and probably from lying in bed for forty days."

"Anyway," She continued talking and pacing. "I ended up downstairs in the emergency room looking for someone to give me an aspirin. I was nearly knocked over when Lisa Bixbee's gurney whizzed past me. That was the first time I saw the dark spirit named Rage. He snatched Lisa's spirit from her body right before my very eyes. That's when Rage realized I could see him. That's why I was so terrified the day I saw him again hanging around Bret Louis.

That spirit links Bret to this crime in someway. I'm just not sure how yet, but I'm thinking that maybe Bret killed Lisa."

With his arm already propped up on the desk, Adam dropped his head into his hands and massaged his temples. "Slow down a minute. You can't accuse Bret without some solid proof. Knapp may be a faith filled judge, but even she can't charge a man because of an angel's hearsay or because you think he did it. Now, will you please sit down? You're wearing out my eyes. Have you been taking pacing lessons from Victor Dillon?" He tried joking to lighten the stress in the room. He was beginning to wish she had never told him about her insight into the spiritual world, or maybe he was sorry she had convinced him to believe her.

The slight grin on Eve's face was an indication that the humor had worked, if even a little. She complied by resuming her seat.

"Eve," Adam started out again on a serious tone. "I've got to admit this is even hard for me to imagine. I believe you're telling me the truth, but I guess I just don't know enough about spiritual things to understand. So did you actually speak to Rachel's angel today?"

"No. But while I was talking to Rachel, Hamuel was talking to Halohesh. An angel can't tell a lie, unless they want to fall into darkness, and then they become…"

"Okay, okay." Adam raised both hands to slow her down. She was a fast talker when she became excited and he was having a hard enough time absorbing things as it was. "This is a little foreign to me. It's been a long time since I've been to church, and even then they didn't exactly teach me about all this spiritual warfare stuff. Just promise me that you won't talk with my client again without me present. And until we have an ounce of solid evidence that points to Bret, this conversation has to remain strictly between us. Promise me that."

"I promise. You are the first and only person I've talked to about this. In fact, you're the only person I *can* talk to about this, since the only other people who believe me are my Aunt and my niece."

Once she found out what time to be at Adam's for dinner, she left his office. Walking home she couldn't help but feel like she needed to go to Southwind Quarter Horse Farms. The same gentle voice that had prompted her to visit Rachel was now directing her to visit Southwind.

Chapter 20

After dinner Eve stayed until it was dark talking to Adam's parents. It was the third time Eve had dinner with them. Besides being very pleasant, they were both very knowledgeable about the Bible, and they both had the light in their eyes, so Eve listened closely to their wisdom.

Adam seemed to enjoy listening to their Bible discussion, but he didn't join in on the conversation. Eve could only hope he was learning while he listened. Although she still hadn't seen a light rekindled in his eyes, she did noticed he was starting to ask questions.

Adam's slim six-foot tall father, Maliciah, was a second-generation cowboy. At sixty his hair was silvery gray, except his sideburns and his bushy brown mustache. He spoke slow and casual as if he had all day to tell a story. And there was a gentleness in his tone that made it a pleasure to listen to him. His face was deeply tanned from long hours in the sun, but his forehead was another story, it was pale from wearing his crunched up old cowboy hat everyday. His deep blue eyes added a friendly softness to his leathery face.

Urma was two years younger than Maliciah and her light brown hair was just beginning to reflect touches of gray at her temples. She was a thin petite woman with a smooth tanned complexion that made her look younger, especially standing next to a husband that was a whole foot taller.

Between talking to Urma and Adam, Eve learned that Urma's mother died when Urma was only fifteen, and that she met Maliciah a year later when he came to work for her father. Maliciah had been the one and only man Urma ever dated or loved, so their marriage was inevitable.

Adam walked out on the front porch with Eve to see her off.

"Boy the stars really do twinkle, don't they?" Eve stared up into the night sky.

"Yes they do." Adam looked up and thought how Eve had a way of showing him things in a refreshing new light, as if he were seeing them for the first time himself. Questions still ran through his mind as he watched her driving away. Curiosity turned him around and sent him back inside his parent's house in hopes of finding some answers.

"We thought you were going home." Urma stopped in the kitchen doorway when she saw Adam come back through the front door. "Is something wrong?"

"Not really, I just wanted to ask a few questions. Do you think it's possible for a person to see and speak to angels?"

Urma shrugged her shoulders. "Sure. All things are possible with God. Daniel saw lots of angels and spoke to them, or heard them, in dreams and visions. God even allowed a donkey to see angels. Remember the story in Numbers of Balaam and how his donkey kept stopping because of the angel in the path?"

"That's right," Adam nodded. "and didn't he even talk to the donkey and hear it talking to him?"

Maliciah nodded his head. "So God could allow anyone to see what he wants. Why are you seeing things?"

"Not me."

"Then who?" Maliciah cleared his throat after questioning.

"Eve told me that when she got her sight that she could see into the spiritual realm as well as the physical. I want to believe her, and I do to an extent, it's just…" Adam sank down into the plump faux suede sofa. Thinking over his words carefully. "…I guess it's just that I didn't think things like this still happened today. I know they used to take place in the Bible days, but…"

"They just don't happen as often nowadays, because there's so many more people and so few who believe. Peoples' faith was a lot stronger back then, so the Spirit of God was freer to work in the world." Maliciah explained. "At least that's how I see it."

Urma finished taking the empty glasses into the kitchen expressing her agreement from the other room. Then she came back into the living room and sat back down in her favorite tan velvet rocker with the worn arms. She had covered the arms with doilies, but the worn threads were still somewhat visible.

"I can't imagine what reason Eve would have for lying about something like that." Urma added, then sent her rocker moving in that peculiar way – with one leg extended forward, while the other leg pumped the chair into a rocking motion. "From what little I've been able to talk with her, she seems like a very honest girl. She's pretty knowledgeable about the Bible too."

Maliciah looked up from his intense search through the Bible to ask a question. "You said she got her sight back after being struck by lightning and then she was in a coma for forty days, is that right?" Once Adam nodded, he continued on with his search into the scriptures.

"Jesus healed a lot of blind people in his days, in a lot of different ways." Urma picked up her knitting and went on. "So why is it so hard for you to believe her Adam?"

"I'm not sure." Adam shrugged. "I somewhat believe her I guess, but I just need solid proof. You know…real evidence. After being a lawyer all these years I just need substantial evidence. Especially when someone tells me they think they know who the real murderer is due to hearsay from an angel."

"Here's the one that I was looking for." Maliciah jumped back into the conversation. "In Psalms twenty nine the seventh verse says, 'The voice of the Lord strikes with flashes of lightning.' Then there's another scripture in Job where God is speaking to Job and asks him, 'Do you send the lightning bolts on their way? Do they report to you, here we are?' He also sent a bright light to blind Paul for three days when he was on the road to Damascus, yet the men that were with him weren't blinded by it. He can use the lightning to work miracles as well as to strike a person dead. So knowing God is in control of the lightning, how can you have doubts? Or is this simply a way to keep her at arms length?"

A scowl creased Adam's brow. "What's that supposed to mean?"

"Let me rephrase the question. Are you starting to fall for the girl? And is this your way of keeping her at a safe distance?"

"I'm not sure of that either. But I guess I wouldn't want to fall in love with someone who's delusional and on her way to the loony bin." Adam stood to leave, since the questions were beginning to get too personal.

A slight smirk touched Urma's lips as she glanced up from her knitting to look at her son's expression. She knew from the look on his face and from the infatuated way Adam had watched Eve all evening, even if he wasn't ready to admit it to anyone, including himself. And why not? Eve was a true natural beauty, inside and out. In fact, she couldn't think of any better match for her son than Eve Kincaid. Even Adam's first wife hadn't been such an ideal match. Adam needed someone who could challenge him and encourage him to grow, which Megan had never done in the twelve years they were married. But in the two short months Adam had spent getting to know Eve, Urma had seen a change and a growth in his curiosity concerning the Bible. So Urma was all for giving Eve her seal of approval. And she sensed that Maliciah felt the same way.

Unseen

"Good night." Adam glanced around the room feeling under the spotlight as he turned to leave. He knew his feelings for Eve were growing, but he wasn't about to admit anything to them yet, not 'til he was sure himself.

Adam had so much on his mind that it was hard to sleep until exhaustion overtook him.

Chapter 21

When Eve got home she was still pondering on a reason to visit Southwind. That night before climbing into bed, she prayed hard for God to give her a believable reason.

By the time the sun rose Saturday morning, Eve had the answer to her prayer. God had given her a dream of being somewhere purchasing a horse of her own, and somehow she knew that ranch was Southwind even though she'd never been there. So after sending a smile and a thank you towards heaven, she climbed out of bed.

She pulled on an old pair of jeans. Tucked in her T-shirt. Then slid her feet into the new pair of riding boots that Adam helped her pick out the previous weekend.

Until riding with Adam, Eve had known nothing about horses, since then she's discovered that she really enjoys riding. In fact, she might even like to have her own horse someday, but not quite yet. So there was no harm in shopping around for one, even if she wasn't exactly ready to buy.

"Are you going riding again with Adam?" Peggy questioned when Eve entered the kitchen. Peggy was already on her second cup of coffee, since she'd woke up before dawn. It still bothered her that Eve was spending so much time with Adam. She had been with him until after nine last night and now she looked as though she was going to spend another weekend riding with him. "We need to take a weekend and go shopping or something. We haven't done that since you gained your eyesight. In fact, we haven't done anything except go out to eat a few times."

Eve shot a thoughtful look at her mother as she dropped some bread into the toaster. "Is that why you've been so grumpy lately?"

"Grumpy?" Peggy scoffed. "Do you think I'm grumpy?"

"A little, yes."

"Well, I guess I am feeling left out." Peggy watched Eve over the rim of her cup as she took another sip. "Since you were born my whole world was wrapped around caring for you. Now that you don't seem to need me at all anymore, I just don't know what to do with myself, and this depression has settled over me." She raised a hand in protest when she saw Eve's lips part to speak. "Now hold on. I have prayed hard and long about it. But I still don't know what to do to get out of this slump. And the more I see you slipping away and wrapping yourself around Adam…"

"Mom." Eve walked up behind her mother and wrapped her arms around her neck. "I'm sorry if I haven't been spending enough time with you lately, I didn't realize that's what I'd been doing. And I'm not going over to Adam's. Actually, I'm going to another ranch to check something out."

"Oh…and what's that dear?"

Eve's toast popped up and gave her the extra time she needed to choose her words. Should she tell her mother the whole reason she was going to Southwind, or just part of it? She could always start out with half, but she knew her mother would end up prying the rest out of her, one way or the other. So Eve made it easy on both of them and just came out and told her the whole plan.

"What?" Peggy cried out with dismay. "You can't seriously be thinking about getting that involved in a trial you're going to be transcribing in a few weeks.

And what if they suspect something and harm you too. This is one of the craziest ideas you've ever had Evelyn Kincaid. You know you're risking your job, don't you? Are you sure they even sell horses there?"

"I shouldn't have told you. Just like I should've told you I could see into the spirit world…"

"So you're going to bring *that* up again. I thought that was over."

"No. I just stopped talking to you about it, because for some reason you can't seem to believe me. Why mom? Is it because you don't think God can still do *those kinds* of miracles anymore?" Eve sat down with her toast and coffee, but suddenly her appetite was gone. She stared across the table at her mother wondering why she wouldn't believe her. "No wonder you're getting depressed. You taught me to never lie, and now you think I'm all of a sudden this big fat liar."

"I never said that Eve."

"Not in words maybe. But that's what it tells me when you don't believe what I'm saying?"

"I'm sorry Eve." Peggy dropped her head into her hands and began to cry. "I guess I've just been thinking all this was too good to last. I was afraid that one morning you'd wake up and it'd all be gone and that you'd be blind again. I was expecting disappointment so badly that I haven't been able to enjoy the blessing."

Eve got up to comfort her mother. Then once they had things worked out, they made plans to go shopping later in the day. Peggy agreed to put her doubts behind her and that she wanted to start enjoying Eve's newly found sight with her.

Eve knew they sold horses at Southwind since Adam had mentioned it once. She thought about things she could say on her drive to the ranch. She wanted to tell her ideas to Hamuel, only he was following her from somewhere outside the car as usual. At least she knew he was going with her, so it gave her the added courage she needed.

When Eve reached the ranch she parked in front of the barn and stepped out of the car. As an overwhelming sense of evil lurking in the shadows hit her, a shiver raised the hairs on her skin.

A Mexican man in a straw cowboy hat was the first one out of the barn to greet her. He wasn't much taller or older than her, but he definitely appeared built for ranch work. His kind face made Eve feel more at ease.

"Mañana señorita. I'm Paco De la Puente at your service. How can I help you?" His voice was well mannered and gentle, although, his speech was too fast for his thick Spanish accent.

Yet Eve managed to absorb every word. "I'm looking to buy a horse. Are you who I need to talk to about that?"

"I can show you what horses are for sale, but you'll need to talk to señor Louis about the prices." Paco turned to head back into the barn. Motioning for her to follow. "You came at a good time, since I was just about to put the horses out to pasture for the day. In here you can get a better look at them."

She followed him through the large doors into a dimly lit breezeway. Another shiver ran the length of her spin as she walked into the shaded interior. It was mid August, one of the hottest months of the year, so she was anything but cold. She knew from Rachel that the murder took place in the barn office. The room to her left was full of saddles and horse tack, so the room to the right had to be the office, since the rest were stalls as far as she could see. The exception being, an opening just past the office that led into a large indoor arena.

"Are you an experienced rider?" Paco questioned over a stocky shoulder.

"Not really. I've just recently learned. But I enjoy it so much I think I'd like one of my own to ride."

"Do you have a place to keep it then? Because señor Louis boards a few horses here too." Paco informed as he stopped in front of a stall. He told her how old the horse was and that he was very well

Unseen

broke, but he thought the price would be very high on that particular gelding. He showed her another gelding and two mares.

When Eve told him that she liked the palomino mare, Paco put a halter on the horse and walked it into the indoor arena for her. He made the horse run circles around him strictly with voice commands. The mare's fluid strides were captivating and nearly made Eve forget she wasn't really there to buy the horse.

Paco informed her that he'd have to go and get señor Louis if she wanted to ride the horse or to know the price. For the sake of curiosity Eve did want to know the price, since she had no idea how much she would need to actually buy a horse, so Paco excused himself to get Mr. Louis from the house.

Eve waited where she was, in the opening between the breezeway that led to the arena. The smell of sawdust and leather filled her senses as she watched the horse still moving freely around the arena. As her eyes followed the mare, she started to notice something strange on the silver tube gate between her and the arena. An area that looked like polished silver. Then as she looked closer she could tell it was a handprint. She compared it to her hand and noted that it was close to the same size, so she placed her hand over it and wrapped her fingers around the rail.

Suddenly Eve's eyesight began to blur. Like a thick black cloud was closing in on her. "Oh God please not now. Please don't take away my sight now. Not here, please not here." She whispered and held on tightly to the rail as a slight dizziness washed over her.

Then just as suddenly, she could see again. Only now there was a different horse in the arena. And the arm she saw was deeply tanned, unlike her own fair skin, so something was wrong. Then she heard someone walking up behind her and turned to see who it was. It was Bret Louis and the dark spirit named Jealousy, both displaying wide smiles. Eve opened her mouth to speak, but it wasn't her words or voice that she heard.

"Don't even think you're gonna watch me ride this crazy horse."

Bret let out a laugh. "Lisa, stop acting like you don't like all the attention. You know you like me watching you."

"Lisa? I'm not Lisa." Eve's mind cried out, but the words never came out. *"God, what's happening to me?"*

Eve turned back to look at the horse in the arena, even though she didn't want to. She didn't want to turn her back to this man or the spirits that followed him. He couldn't be trusted. But it was as if she wasn't in control anymore. Could she possibly be seeing a memory from Lisa's body? But why, and how? Lisa was dead.

Bret's hands gripped both of her shoulders firmly from behind. "When are you gonna admit you want me as much as I want you?" Bret's voice jeered over her shoulder. Inches from her ear. Close enough to feel the warmth of his breath.

Eve wanted to scream or run, but instead laughter is the sound she heard. It had to be Lisa's laughter, not her own, since the sound was alien to her own ears.

"Only in your dreams Bret." Lisa laughed again. "In your dreams."

Then suddenly she felt a crushing pain in her neck as his teeth sunk into her flesh. A muffled scream was trapped in her throat as she squirmed to get free. But the vise like grip on her shoulders held her.

Even in her transfixed state, Eve's acute hearing was still active. She could hear someone's footsteps as they stopped at the corner behind them, she even got a fait smell of after-shave before they turned and left.

Eve jerked her hand free from the rail when she heard the sound of swords crashing together. Once again her eyes blurred and then slowly came back into focus. With her heart racing she quickly looked around to see who was behind her. To her surprise, no one was there, and the barn was as silent as before – with the exception of her labored breathing and Hamuel battling with Rage in the arena.

The horse was running and snorting wildly as if it could sense the battle taking place.

From behind her in the breezeway she could hear Paco talking to someone. When she turned this time, Bret and Paco were walking towards her. Thankfully this time Bret wasn't grinning from ear to ear.

"Eve. We meet again." Bret proffered a hand towards her.

This time she accepted his outstretched hand. Even though the image of him biting Lisa's neck flashed through her mind.

"You've got excellent taste. This is one of our best mares." He propped a boot up on the lower rail of the gate, and folded his arms over the top of the gate in a very natural manor. "Course she'll run ya about ten thousand."

Eve's mouth draped open. "Ten thousand dollars?"

Bret smiled and gave a quick nod. "Yep."

"Then I guess I'm going to have to save up a lot more money before I can buy a horse of my own."

Both men let out a soft chuckle.

"We do have a two year-old that you can buy for about three thousand." Bret offered.

"That's still a little more than I was counting on right now."

"Well, let me get you a business card and when you get the money or change your mind give us a call. My dad is usually good about letting people make payments until they get a horse paid off, but it'll have to stay here until it's paid for."

"Okay." Eve was ready to get out of there after the pulse-racing episode she experienced. Behind her she could hear Hamuel's sword still clashing with the dark angel's sword, so she hoped to help him out as well by leaving.

"I'm going to put the horses out." Paco said with amusement still lingering in his deep brown eyes. He walked off whistling without waiting for a response.

She followed Bret to the office. She was concerned about being alone with Bret now that she knew he was the one who bit Lisa on the neck. And most likely he was the one who killed her too, because of her continued rejection of him.

Eve stopped just outside the office door. She was afraid to step in there with him. Instead she watched him from the doorway. His brow creased as he dug through every desk drawer to find a business card without luck. Then he lifted the desk calendar and pulled a thin stationary tablet out from under it. Tearing off the top sheet, he walked it over to her.

"I couldn't find the business cards and I know dad just got a new box. Anyway, this has our name, address and phone number on the letterhead, so take this." He handed the paper over to her. "Doesn't Adam have any horses for sale at his place?"

"I haven't asked him yet, but I don't think he does." She admitted honestly.

Eve took the paper and folded it in half. Then she was quick to thank him and walk out to her car. At that instant, she noticed the dark spirit escape through the roof of the barn with Hamuel close behind. She watched to see if Hamuel saw her in the car as she leaned over to put the paper in her glove box. When Hamuel noticed Eve's car pulling away from the barn, he stopped his pursuit to follow her.

Chapter 22

Eve headed directly to Eden's ranch from Southwind. She had to tell Adam what she experienced. During the short drive she determined that the handprint she'd seen and touched must have been Lisa's, since the vision was from Lisa's perspective. Another thing Eve determined, someone had witnessed the incident between Lisa and Bret. But who? It couldn't have been Rachel, since it was a man's after-shave she had smelled. So who was it?

As Eve pulled up in front of Adam's apartment, she saw him leaning on his balcony rail drinking a cup of coffee. The double doors behind him were both standing wide open. There was a set of stairs leading to the balcony, as well as a set of stairs leading to the apartment from inside the garage, so her obvious choice was the balcony stairs.

A smile brightened Adam's stubble ridden cheeks. Even with his ruffled uncombed hair he was attractive. She diverted her eyes from his face, and immediately wished she hadn't. She blushed at the sight of his unbuttoned shirt, not because it was the first hairy chest she'd ever seen, but from the desire to touch it that stirred within her.

"Sorry." Adam quickly apologized once he remembered his open shirt. He sat his cup on the wood rail while he buttoned up his shirt. "I wasn't expecting company. Did we make plans to ride this morning that I forgot about?"

"No. I just needed to talk with you about what I saw this morning at Southwind." She began somewhat breathless.

"Southwind." Adam echoed in frustration. "What were you doing at Southwind?"

"I went there looking to buy a horse."

"Really?" Adam frowned. "I didn't know you wanted to buy a horse. I've got one I'd sell you at a better price then they'd want."

Eve raised a protesting hand. "I don't exactly want to buy one yet. Something just kept telling me to go there to see what I could see for myself. Anyway, Paco put a horse in the indoor arena for me to look at, and then he went to get Bret. Well, while

I was waiting, I noticed this strange image on the gate. It was luminous like the moon. It was the size of a handprint, so I put mine up to it to compare the size. When my hand was almost an exact fit, I placed mine over the other. Then the strangest thing happened. I got a vision or something. Only it was like I was seeing through Lisa's eyes. I saw and heard what transpired up to the moment she was bit on the neck. I know who bit her neck, and I know that someone witnessed it, but I don't know who."

"Wait a minute. Let me get this straight. You know who bit her, but you don't know who saw it happen?" A bewildered look filled his eyes. "And how do you know it was Lisa?" Before giving her a chance to answer he took her by the arm and ushered her inside the door. "I think we'd better sit down and talk this over more slowly."

Adam fixed Eve a cup of coffee without asking if she even wanted one. Putting sugar and vanilla creamer in it the way she liked it. Then he sat down across from her at the small table just inside the double doors.

Eve went over the story with him once more. Slower, since she'd regained her breath. She explained how she heard Bret call Lisa's name, and how she'd seen Bret's face. Then how the witness was someone she only heard and smelled behind them,

Unseen

but she didn't see a face. She also told him that she saw the dark spirit there again.

"I can't believe you're getting this involved in this case. You're not a detective. This is highly irregular you know? It could even get you thrown off the trial as the reporter if you're not careful. Not to mention it's just plain crazy for you to be investigating things, *especially* on your own like this." Adam wasn't sure if he should be angry with her for going, or glad that she didn't get harmed in any way. "This is still not going to convince a judge to bring Bret in as a suspect."

Eve didn't expect to be scolded by him. It left her wide-eyed and speechless.

Adam leaned over the table and cradled her face between both of his hands. "I don't want anything bad to happen to you girl. Don't you know that? You've got to stop running with these wild notions of yours. I've come to know how much you like a challenge, but promise me you won't do anymore snooping on this case."

"I've always got protection." Eve reached out with one hand and touched the rough whiskers on his cheek. "Oh." She smiled and flinched at the first initial feel of the roughness on her sensitive fingertips. Then she let her fingers move slowly over the texture with delight. "Your whiskers are very coarse."

As Adam's eyes passed over the fullness of her lips a sudden urge to kiss her filled his senses. Just as suddenly he withdrew his hands and sat back in his chair so that her hand could no longer reach his face. Then he rubbed his cheek where her hand had been in an attempt to rub away the sensation her touch left behind.

For a moment Eve wondered if his reaction was because he didn't want her touching him. Was it because he hadn't shaved? Was it her touch? Maybe he just didn't like being touched. Or perhaps she was reading too much into it. Since she still wasn't used to reading peoples facial expressions she couldn't be sure what to think.

"Yes, I know." He offered a weary smile. "I'm surprised you haven't noticed I need a shower too. I was up late looking over Rachel's case, and then I started back in again this morning. I had only stopped long enough to make coffee and take a short break when you pulled up."

Eve stayed long enough to drink her coffee. She had to turn down his offer to go horseback riding, since she'd promised to spend some time with her mother.

On her drive home she wondered again about Adam's sudden withdrawal from her touch.

Eve spent the rest of the day with her mother shopping. They stopped long enough to eat lunch and dinner. This was the first time Eve was able to pick out her own clothes without asking her mother to describe them to her. Eve had fun trying on different dresses and seeing how they looked on her, but Peggy found out just how picky her daughter was. Out of a dozen dresses, at five different stores, Eve decided on only three.

Peggy, on the other hand, bought about a dozen new outfits, averaging two from every store. It was at the most expensive store, Raymond's Department store, where she bought the most – four outfits. Simply being in the store caused her to think of Mrs. Chadwick and her shoplifting due to the high prices.

Eve hadn't known her mother to be so quick to spend her money before, so of course, she questioned it. Peggy explained that she had lost weight while Eve was in the hospital and now everything was too baggy on her. She also admitted that Raymond's had the best quality, so she hoped they would last her a great deal longer than a cheaper quality.

But Eve still didn't see it fitting into her mother's natural character. Since Eve's father had been a doctor, they never had a financial struggle, even with putting two sons through college and a daughter through trade school. Yet growing up Eve had

Unseen

always known her mother to spend every dime wisely. Which may have been the reason they were able to put two boys through college. Even their home was an elegant yet modest two-story town house when it could have been much more. So Eve couldn't help but wonder if the spending had something to do with her mother's depression.

Chapter 23

Sunday morning Eve woke up feeling good. Like she'd had the most refreshing nights' sleep she'd ever had. Then after breakfast and a shower, she put on one of her new outfits. A sage green broomstick skirt that had tiny pink roses all over it, a matching pink blouse, topped off with a form fitting sage vest. Her riding boots completed the look of the outfit nicely. It not only complimented her green eyes, but her complexion as well.

'Adam would like this.' The thought ran through her mind so fast, that she had to wonder if it actually came from her. Just as quickly she brushed it off and went into the living room to see if her mother was ready to go.

"My that does look lovely on you dear." Peggy stopped the motion of her rocker as she commented and looked her daughter over. "I've already called Lexi, so she'll be ready to go when we get there."

"Then let's go if you're ready," Eve noted the new outfit her mother had on, so she complimented her as well. "and I can see you are from your radiant appearance."

With a smile Peggy grabbed her Bible and followed Eve to the back door.

Shadow rubbed against Eve's leg with a whimper. Eve bent over to pet the dog's head. "Sorry girl, you have to stay here. I know you're used to going everywhere with me and that I've been neglecting you a little too, but you don't need to go with me now. I know you don't understand. I wish you could."

"We don't want to be late dear." Peggy urged.

With a heavy sigh Eve walked through the door. She was beginning to realize that she'd not only been neglecting her mother, but her dog as well. The one companion that had offered her so much love and security over the past ten years.

Peggy was talking to Eve as Lexi walked up to the passenger side of the car. Eve didn't hear a single word her mother said. All she could do was watch her niece approaching. All she could hear was a voice in her head singing hallelujah as she saw the light gleaming in Lexi's denim blue eyes.

Eve's eyes glazed over with tears of joy. The instant Peggy saw the look on Eve's face, she stopped talking and turned her head to see what Eve was looking at. Lexi had a bright smile on her face, but there didn't appear to be anything out of the ordinary about her, at least nothing that should cause Eve to nearly cry.

"What is it Eve? What's wrong?" Peggy questioned in a soft voice.

"She's got the light in her eyes." Eve whispered over the lump in her throat as Lexi reached the car door.

"You gonna let me in gra'ma?"

"Sure sweetie." Peggy opened the door and stepped out to let Lexi climb up in the middle of the front seat.

"So you did it, didn't you?" In anticipation Eve leaned over closer to Lexi.

Lexi simply nodded her head with a sheepish smile that lit up her face.

"Did what? What are you two mumbling about?" Peggy couldn't stand the suspense.

"I asked Jesus into my heart last night." Lexi tilted her head up gleefully.

"Oh...he's there baby girl, he's there." Eve assured them in an elated tone of voice. Her broad smile was even more elated as she hugged her niece. "Now we've just got to keep working on your mommy and daddy to get the light back in their eyes."

From the look on Eve's face and the confidence in her voice, Peggy knew that Eve had definitely seen something in Lexi's eyes. A Light, she had said. A light that apparently wasn't in her parents' eyes.

For the first time since this all began in July, Peggy began to believe, and her heart streamed with joy. Eve must have been given a very special gift when she was granted the miracle of sight.

The car pulled away from the curb, but Peggy's thoughts remained fixed on the look in Eve's eyes. Angelic compassion was the only words Peggy could think of to describe the look she saw in her daughter's green eyes.

Eve looked up at the halo of angels surrounding the church when she stepped out of the car. Then she whispered her thanks to the Lord.

"Eve."

A familiar voice called out across the parking lot. Was it? Her heart raced to think it could be, then she turned, and saw that it was Adam. He waved to her as he climbed out of his jeep. He had actually taken her up on her countless invitations to join them at church. *Glory...what a day!* Her heart cried out. A look of disbelief was written all over Peggy's face when Eve shot her a quick glance.

"Will miracles never cease?" Peggy found her voice. She'd been speechless since leaving Keith's house after picking up Lexi.

Adam smiled at Peggy then Eve as he reached them. "Good morning ladies. And might this be little Lexi whom I've heard so much about?" He bent over slightly to proffer a hand towards the girl. In his mind he summed up that she was about the same age his son would have been.

"I am." Lexi confirmed as she shook his hand. "Are you here to ask Jesus into your heart too? I asked him into mine last night and I feel happier today." She looked up with innocent eyes waiting on his hesitant reply.

Adam let out a slightly uneasy laugh. "Someday I suppose I will."

"What's wrong with today?" Lexi crunched up her forehead in confusion.

"Lexi." Eve scolded. "He will when he's ready. No one pressured you, so you shouldn't pressure Adam." Diverting her attention back to Adam, she asked, "You are going to sit with us, aren't you?"

"Of course. I'd be honored to sit with three lovely ladies." Adam showed off his pearly white teeth with a bright smile. His eyes drank in a quick approval of Eve's new outfit, thinking how perfectly it suited her.

Unseen

Eve had seen him in suits plenty of times before, but for some reason he looked sharper than usual. Maybe it was just due to the fact that he had came to church. Maybe it was the hope she had in him.

Chapter 24

The following morning Peggy drove to her sister's farm to express her concerns about Eve's involvement in the murder investigation. Since Maggy had been a court reporter, and still substituted when needed, Peggy knew she'd have some good advice.

Maggy put up her gardening tool and listened thoughtfully until Peggy had finished. "Don't worry too much Peg, I'm sure she'll use good judgement. Besides, if she gets too involved, they'll simply pull her as the reporter and call me in to take her place. I'm sure she knows that, so she's not going to risk it if this case means so much to her. The best thing we can do is keep her lifted up in prayer." Rising off the porch swing she asked. "Would you like a glass of lemonade?"

"Sure." Peggy responded without breaking the rhythm of the swing.

Maggy returned with two glasses of fresh lemonade and sat back down, again, without breaking the rhythm of the swing. As young girls they had perfected the art of popping off and on the porch swing without breaking a single stride.

"I know it all has to do with this new found gift she has for seeing things…"

Maggy flashed a sideward glance at her sister. "Well, it's about time you start believing in her."

"I was finally convinced yesterday when we picked Lexi up for church. Eve knew Lexi had made a commitment to God before she told us about it. She saw the light in Lexi's eyes, and from the look on Eve's face…I knew she'd seen something."

"That must have been exciting. I'm happy for Lexi. Now we've got someone else to help us work on Keith and Lou Ann."

Peggy's face paled. "That's right. Eve did say that there was no light in their eyes, or Troy and Debbie's." The short hairs on Peggy's spine stood up at the chilling revelation. Her daughter was truly gifted with something unique. Yet something that must also feel like a heavy burden, to know that someone she loved wasn't saved.

Unseen

Maggy saw the dismay on Peggy's face. "Do you see now why she needs your support more than ever?" Peggy managed a weak nod before Maggy continued. "She needs you to help her pray, to help her find answers in the scriptures, but most of all she needs you to listen."

Peggy stayed and had lunch with Maggy and Alex before driving back to town. Their discussion concerning Eve had been eye opening as well as helpful. Peggy had a new purpose. A new mission to perform in her daughter's life. She had thought that her daughter no longer needed her, but now she saw just how wrong she was.

Maggy had also informed Peggy about a few things that Eve revealed to her when she was teaching her how to drive. Things about her childhood that Eve couldn't possibly have known. Stories that neither Maggy nor Peggy had ever spoken of to anyone accept each other in over forty years.

"As a test one day, I asked Eve to tell me what I'd dreamed that night, and after conferring with my angel, she told me exactly what I had dreamed. Then she even went on to tell me what it meant. She interpreted it, just like Daniel would have." Maggy's words were still echoing through Peggy's mind when she arrived home.

"Lord forgive me for being so selfish." Peggy looked to the sky as she stepped out of the car. "I've been feeling so sorry for myself that I couldn't rejoice in the miracle that was right under my nose. Too selfish to be happy for someone else's joy. Help me know how to make it up to her, please." With a glance at her watch, she saw that Eve would be home in less than hour. Once inside she began preparing one of Eve's favorite meals, broiled salmon with steamed broccoli and snap peas.

Over dinner Peggy told Eve about the reoccurring dream she was still having, where she keeps finding Eve burnt on the floor with her eyes opened and blazing.

Eve told Peggy what she thought it meant. "Well the last verse of Hebrews twelve says our God is a consuming fire. So I think God might have been trying to show you how he consumed my blindness and opened my eyes to things seen and unseen."

Somehow Peggy knew Eve had interpreted the dream correctly. Like the light had come on. It also showed her that Eve knew the scriptures better than she realized.

Chapter 25

It had been a week since Dixon was last at Southwind, yet he was there once more to talk to Paco. It had bothered him long enough. He had to find out if Paco could tell him what might have been sitting in the breezeway that night, since he hadn't wrote anything about it in his report. Which must have seemed too insignificant at the time. So why should it bother him now? Details. He needed all the details.

Dixon stopped his car in front of the barn and climbed out of the cool AC into the dry August heat. Temperatures soaring well over the one hundred mark. Making him wish he could have done this task from the cool comfort of his office. He didn't hesitate in taking off his suit jacket and tossing it in over the back of his seat. It exposed his shoulder holster, but it was better than creating a major sauna under his arms.

"Ah, señor Dixon. I thought I heard someone pull up." Paco emerged from the barn with a friendly smile. He respectfully wiped his hand on his bandanna before proffering it towards the detective. "Good afternoon."

"Afternoon señor De la Puente." Dixon returned with a firm handshake. "Looks like they've been working you hard this morning."

"Sí señor. I just finished cleaning stalls." Paco lifted his straw hat to wipe the sweat from his brow, using the bandanna in his hand. He turned to look back down the breezeway of the barn. "There's seven stalls in the barn, and seven more along the eastside of the indoor arena. It keeps me in shape."

Dixon followed him inside the barn thinking you'd have to be in shape to keep from passing out in the heat. The shade was a slight relief from the scorching sun. He followed Paco just beyond the office to the opening that led to the indoor arena. They stopped at the opened gate to look at the stalls on the eastside Paco referred to.

With the doors opened on the south and west sides of the arena, the sunlight streamed in and pointed it out like a beacon. There it was. The very thing Dixon came looking for. With all the sunlight on it, it looked bigger, but he was almost sure that was it. The very object he saw in the breezeway that night. Only he didn't remember it being hooked to a tractor. Now he didn't even have to think about how to ask Paco about the unidentified object.

"What is that?" Dixon pointed in the direction he was looking.

"That's the manure spreader, why?" Paco gave Dixon a baffled look. "Haven't you ever seen one before?"

"Only once and it wasn't hooked up to a tractor then, I saw it the night Lisa was murdered, it was in the breezeway then wasn't it? I just didn't know what it was called. Is it usually parked in the breezeway?"

Paco shook his head. "Señor Louis doesn't like it inside the barn unless someone is cleaning stalls. It's usually kept out on the eastside of the barn. In fact, I remember how mad señor Louis was about it being left in here. He was especially mad because he had to dump it himself, since I was kept in jail." Paco took a breath to continue, but stopped when he heard Dixon's cell phone ring.

George raised a finger towards Paco as he reached for his phone. "Dixon here." He walked back to the entrance of the barn to get better reception. Todd began telling him about the DNA results on the second polyester fiber. It matched the fiber found on the victim's body, the blood was a match to the victim, and there were traces of gun-powered residue on it – adding to Woodrow's theory about the pillow being used to muffle the shot.

"Well I've got some good news myself." Dixon informed. "I found the object I was looking for. But I'm not sure if it has any significance in the case or not."

"Never leave any stone unturned. What did it turn out to be?"

Dixon let out a soft chuckle. "A manure spreader."

Todd chuckled back through the phone. "Well if it does turn out to have any significance, call another criminalist to search it for evidence, will ya?"

Dixon laughed again. "Not a chance. You're my man all the way."

By the time George was off the phone Paco was no where to be found, so he got back into his car to leave. After all, he had the information he'd came to get, which wasn't worth the weight it could carry. All it did was ease the load on his mind and added that final detail he thought he needed. Yet he was left wondering which, señor Louis, Paco was referring to, Bret or Herb, or if it was even relevant.

When he started the car, he cranked the AC up on high, and pointed all the vents on him before pulling away from the barn. Wishing once again that he could have done this from his office. Only he knew it was something he had to see to recognize, so it wasn't something he could see from his office. It was a long drive for a little information, but he felt better now that all his stones were turned. He just wished it had been a lead instead of a forgotten detail.

Chapter 26

Two weeks had past when Eve was prompted back to Southwind. On the drive out she was so busy trying to think of what to say, that she didn't notice the dark clouds moving in from the northwest. She figured she'd find Paco in the barn like she did the last time, so she planned on telling Paco that she wanted to see the horse again, and that she needed to talk with Mr. Louis about payment options.

Pulling up in front of the barn, she finally noticed the ominous dark clouds hanging over head, but she wasn't about to let fear stop her now. Even if this was the first storm she could recall since coming out of the coma. She had never feared storms before, why start now? Yet she couldn't deny the uneasiness stirring within her, wondering if God would take her gift away the same way he had given it, by striking her once more with lightning.

No one was in the barn when Eve walked through calling out. There wasn't anyone in the arena either. So Eve went to the office to see if anyone was in there. She hesitated outside the door before knocking. When no one answered, she opened the door and stepped in the doorway.

A cold chill ran up her spin and stopped her in her tracks she was unable to let go of the doorknob or move her feet. Looking down her eyes began to blur, just like the last time. "Please Lord, not again. Not now." She steadied herself on the doorknob.

She caught a glimpse of a dark stain on the wooden floor when a rumble of thunder snapped her head up. She looked towards the window behind the desk waiting for the lightning that she knew would follow. When the lightning did occur, like a camera flash, she saw Lisa Bixbee sitting at the desk writing on something.

With another flash of lightning, came another image of Lisa looking up. Just before the thunder rumbled Eve heard Lisa speaking to someone. *"I was just writing you a letter."*

With another flash of lightning and rumble of thunder came another snapshot vision. A man standing in front of the desk asked, *"What for, I'm right here?"*

Eve couldn't see who the man was, since his back was to her. From the dark brown hair color and build, she guessed it was Bret, since Paco's complexion was much darker. The vision was in short fragmented snapshots with every flash of lightning. Just before the rain began hitting the tin roof of the barn Eve caught a faint whiff of the same after-shave she smelled the last time she had a vision. "God, why couldn't you let me see through Lisa's eyes again instead of these fragments of information?" Eve whispered. "Let me see who this man is."

"I wasn't sure how else to tell you I'm pregnant." Lisa confessed in another rumble of thunder that followed a flash.

Another rumble was quickly proceeded by a flash to reveal the man holding a gun up to Lisa's abdomen while she clutched a pillow to herself like a feeble shield. Eve's heart began to race with fear. She wasn't sure if it was due to the escalating storm or the tension between Lisa and what was obviously her killer.

The dark spirit Rage suddenly appeared next to the killer. Rage dug his talons into the man's head and began telling him, *"She's been playing you for a fool... kill her... kill her...shut her up forever..."*

The next fragmented image Eve received was another dark spirit, the one Hamuel had called Jealousy, and he was shouting out from the other side of the killer. "She's a filthy lying cheat…you know you're not the only man she's been with…she's a cheat…"

Rain pelted the tin roof so hard that it sounded more like hail. Every flash of lightning and rumble of thunder brought another fragmented picture right up to the gunshot and Lisa falling to the floor.

"What can I do for you señorita Kincaid?"

Paco's voice jolted Eve out of her trance back into reality. Yet she was still a little disoriented when she turned around to look at him. Blinking vigorously until her eyes could focus on him.

"I just noticed your car here. I was inside my home eating lunch." Paco studied her pale face for a moment through narrowed eyes. "Are you all right señorita?"

"Yes… I guess I'm just a little bothered by the storm. I was looking for señor Louis. I wanted to ask him about a payment plan on that horse."

"I'm not sure he's here. Let me go check. I'll be right back."

Once Paco was gone Eve turned back around and prayed to receive more of the vision. When it did resume, the killer was wiping down the gun with a red bandanna, and then returning it to the wall mount above the door. Then he picked up the casing, the pillow, and the crumpled up stationary page. The next fragment Eve saw was the killer stuffing everything inside the hole in the pillow as he turned and ran towards the back of the barn instead of going out the front doors.

At that point Paco returned and interrupted her vision once more. "Señor Herb and señor Bret took some horses to a sale and won't be home until late tomorrow. Can I get a number where they can call you?"

"Ah…that's okay. I'll get back with them when the weather is better." Eve was too disturbed by the vision she had to want to stay a moment longer, she was ready to run away just like the killer had, only in the other direction. "Thank you for your help señor De la Puente."

"Sí señorita. Adiós." Paco walked Eve to her car holding a rain slicker over her, then he headed back over to the first of the two trailers that sat across from the barn.

Chapter 27

The rain was still coming down hard as she pulled out and slowly headed north to highway 56. The rain had let up only slightly by the time she stopped at the intersection to the highway. But her heart started racing all over again when she saw Adam's white jeep coming up the road towards her. Judging from his direction she guessed he was headed into town.

His jeep slowed as he recognized her car and he turned to pull up beside her. He rolled his window down just enough to talk through the opening. "What are you doing out this way?" Adam asked when she cracked her window to hear him.

Eve lowered her eyes. She knew he wasn't going to like hearing what she was about to say. "I was at Southwind looking for more…"

"Eve," Adam's tone was scolding. "I thought you promised…"

"Actually, I never promised anything. I simply told you that I always had protection with me. Remember?"

Adam thought back to the scene at his small table when she had touched his face. With a single touch she had thrown his thoughts so far off track that he had failed to get her promise. He also knew she was a professional listener after seven years of being a court reporter. "I guess your right."

The rain finally came to an end, so Eve rolled the window down all the way. "I had another vision while I was there. This time it was different."

The color drained slightly from Adam's face. "Let's head back to my place and talk. If you've got time." He was still upset with her for going back out there alone, but he repressed it. For now he'd settle on being thankful she was all right.

Eve simply nodded her head and turned towards Eden's Ranch. In her rearview mirror she saw Adam make a U-turn in the road to follow her. Wherever he had planned on going wasn't as important as hearing what she had to say. It gave her a warm feeling to know that Adam cared enough to hear what happened, and that his main concern was for her safety.

Once they were there and settled down at the table with a glass of tea, Eve told him everything.

"So if indeed Lisa was pregnant, then we've got a whole new motive and possible suspect." Adam raised an interested brow. "It's just too bad you never got to see the man's face."

"That's what she was writing to tell him..." Suddenly it dawned on her. "Oh Adam, I may have something else." Eve exclaimed in excitement as she jumped up and rushed out to her car. She dug through her glove box until she found it, there it was, the stationary page.

Adam was curiously watching her from his balcony. She was slowly running her finger over a piece of paper. "What on earth are you doing now?"

"There's an impression on here left from the letter Lisa was writing that night. I can feel the words, but..."

"If that's evidence then you need to stop touching it. The oils in your fingers might damage the evidence." Adam warned.

Eve held the paper up by one corner. "What should I do with it?"

Adam went inside for a minute and returned with a large tan envelope. "Put it in here. I'll take it to Dixon first thing Monday morning." Adam said as he hurried down the steps. They met at the bottom step. He held open the envelope while Eve dropped it in.

"Do you suppose they can still process it?" She questioned.

"Let's pray they can."

An ultra thin smile creased her lips at Adam's acknowledgement of prayer. She may not yet see a light within his eyes, but she has seen a change and heard the hope in his voice. It was almost the flip side, since normally she would have been the optimist, and Adam would have been the one to question.

"Do you have to wait until Monday to get it to him? Because the hearing does start Monday, remember?"

"Well, I suppose if I could get it to him now he might be able to get it to the lab. Only I think the lab is closed on Sundays, so they wouldn't get to it until Monday anyway." He explained.

"But at least they'd have it first thing Monday to get started on."

Now her optimism brought a thin smile to his face. "That's providing they could get to it that fast."

"Let's pray they can." She smiled back and grabbed him by the hand. She started towards her car, but he redirected her towards his jeep.

"I'll drive. Then after we drop this off we can get a bite to eat, since that's where I was headed when I ran into you."

Eve's belly rumbled out an agreement as she fastened her seatbelt.

"That sounded like a yes to me." He smiled over at her as he fastened his own seatbelt. Adam used his cell phone to call ahead to the police station to see if Dixon was even there, which he wasn't, so he tried him at home. After offering a brief explanation George was anxious to see the evidence.

"Sure, bring it right over. My golf game was rained out, it's too wet to Bar-B-Q, and the wife's gone shopping for the day. Driving to Great Bend today sounds better than sitting around a gloomy house alone all day."

"Why don't you meet us at the Brushfire for lunch, if you haven't eaten yet, and I'll buy you lunch for doing this."

"You always were the man with the plan Webber. I'll be there in ten minutes."

"Then save us a seat, we'll be there in fifteen."

Dixon was about to ask who the 'we' was that Adam kept referring to, but Adam hung up before he got the chance. It wasn't long before he had an answer. Adam strolled in five minutes behind him with Evelyn Kincaid on his arm like a charm. He had to admit they were a more striking couple than

Adam and Megan had been. Dixon offered a bold grin and a soft chuckle as they sat down across from him. "You sly fox. You didn't tell me you were seeing someone."

Adam choked up, not quite sure what to say. "Ah…well…I…"

"Seeing someone?" Eve jumped in to help him out. "Define what you mean by that, because frankly, I'm seeing everyone now days."

Her curve ball threw George off for a few minutes, until he thought about it, then he chuckled again. "Yah, I get ya. Okay you got me. I heard about you getting your sight after being struck by lightning. So I guess all that's still working normally?"

"Of course." She confirmed as she placed her napkin over her lap. "God didn't give me a temporary miracle." Eve swallowed hard; hoping she wouldn't be swallowing her own words later, if the gift was indeed temporary as Hamuel said it could be. In any case, it pleased her to give God the glory, especially to someone without the light in his eyes.

Adam had time to gain his thoughts and offered an answer to Dixon. He explained that they were just friends and that they weren't exactly dating. Only the thin smile Dixon offered Adam told him that he wasn't totally buying into his explanation. Having known each other since grade school, he knew Dixon was reading between the lines. It was a wonder that Adam made such a good lawyer when some people could read him all too easy. Which was the reason he always had to find firm ground to build his cases on.

Over lunch they had to give Dixon some details on how they obtained the new evidence. Dixon didn't exactly like how they got it, but at least it wasn't illegally obtained, since Bret had willingly given it to Eve. But it did stand a chance of drawing Eve in as a witness on the case, which would get her pulled from her reporter position if the judge got wind of things.

During the drive over Adam had warned Eve not to mention her vision, but to stick to physical evidence. So they merely told Dixon how they thought Lisa might have been pregnant. Before leaving Dixon promised to let Adam know as soon as he heard anything.

Chapter 28

$\mathcal{D}$ixon ran into Todd Woodrow just as he was about to leave the lab. He filled him in on the new evidence that he had. He expressed the urgency of the information, since Adam would need it for court by eleven Monday morning.

Todd assured Dixon. "I'll stay and run the test on the ESDA myself, and I'll have something for you ASAP"

"Just FAX the results so I can get a copy to A-d-a-m." Dixon teased by spelling out fax and Adam, since Todd had used so many abbreviations in his statement. After a good laugh Dixon thanked him and headed back to Dodge City. All the way there and back he kept trying to figure out how Eve had so quickly convinced him of Rachel's innocence. It kept bringing him back to one thing, her strong confidence. Which lead him to another thought, if she could change his opinion in a single afternoon, she'd eventually change Adam's opinion about them being a couple.

He arrived home just as his wife was unloading shopping bags from her car. Being the loving husband and father that he was, he helped her in with the bags.

"Where'd you go?" Katrina questioned with a kiss. "I tried your cell phone once, but it gave me that out of area message."

"Yeah, I was probably in one of those dead zones. I ran some new evidence up to the lab for Adam." He paused to hold the door open to let his wife enter first. "Do you know who he's hanging out with these days?"

"Evelyn Kincaid. Why?" Then a thought brought a frown to her brow. "What are you doing working on Saturday anyway? I thought you were going to play golf."

"I got rained out." He shrugged, as if it were no big deal, even though he had been looking forward to a relaxing game of golf all week. "You mean you knew about Adam and Eve, and you didn't say anything?"

Katrina laughed as she sat her bags down on the couch. "Gee George, you're suppose to be the detective here, and you didn't know they've been going to lunch nearly everyday, since she left the hospital." She laughed again. "Are you that far behind the times? Besides, hasn't everyone heard about Adam and Eve by now? If not then you need to get back to reading your Bible." She teased with a smile.

He dropped his bags down next to hers and grabbed her playfully around the waist with a smile. "I guess I'm going to have to get me a better informant, since my own wife don't keep me posted anymore. And what's worse is you work for Adam, so is that where your true loyalties lay?" He kissed her neck, first on one side, then on the other. "Am I going to have to start paying you to rat out your boss?"

"Keep kissing me like that and I'll tell you what ever you want Baby."

Their twelve-year-old, Greg, walked through the door with more bags. "Come on you two. The door is wide open. It's bad enough that Tina and me have to see you guys acting like that, but don't make the neighbors suffer too."

They both laughed at his comment and the face that followed.

Then Katrina corrected Greg's grammar. "It's Tina and I dear."

"Just wait son. In a few more years you'll be begging some pretty little girl to kiss you." Dixon responded. "Then I'll be the one busting up the scene."

"Yuck. No way dude." Greg made a revolting face at the thought. He wasn't into girls yet. He still thought they all had cooties and if they couldn't play basketball they weren't even worth talking to.

Dixon had a great relationship with his wife and kids, when he was home long enough to give them his time. But lately with two murder investigations going, he hasn't had much left to give them.

Since the rain had stopped George decided to grill up a nice thick steak for his family and have a good meal together. Maybe make it a family game night or rent a couple videos and watch movies together.

Chapter 29

Woodrow arrived in Dodge City around 10:40 and rushed the results from the letter into Dixon. He handed George the paper that was now in a clear protective jacket; to preserve it from smudges during handling. "Read that and see if you don't think it will change the course of this trial."

With a quick scan Dixon could see that it would bring a definite change to things. "I've got to get this to Adam right away. He's probably already in the courtroom waiting for the hearing to open." Even as he spoke he was heading towards the door.

Dixon rushed across the street to the courthouse, with Woodrow right behind him, and they managed to catch Adam just outside the courtroom. Adam did his own quick read of the letter before entering and presenting it to the prosecuting attorney, Tracy Powers; who was not pleased with the new evidence, especially since it presented itself as a proverbial wrench in her spokes.

"How long have you been withholding this information Webber?" Tracy chastised. "You know this is highly unethical, don't you?"

"Yes, and I'm sorry, but this isn't some sneaky tactic. I received the letter this Saturday, and I didn't know forensics' would have it processed so quickly. I did try to call you Saturday, but I couldn't reach you at either number."

Tracy took a deep-exasperated breath. "I'll just have to work through it. Luckily I still have more against her than you do to defend her. Just see that nothing else like this pops up again while I'm at the lake for the weekend. Okay?"

"Sure thing." Adam agreed with a cordial handshake. Taking his seat, he scanned the benches behind him to make sure Dixon and Woodrow had stuck around, since they were the only witnesses he had to call on. Wait a minute, there was one more, the EMS worker Lisa had mumbled to about a child.

Unseen

Eve got her stenograph machine set up and ready for transcribing. Trying hard to ignore the fact that Adam was bent over Tracy Powers talking all too long and all too closely. As hard as she tried to shake off the jealous feelings that bombarded her, she couldn't.

Tracy Powers was in her early forty's, yet her petite build made her look twenty years younger. Her caramel brown hair was curled under at the shoulder, and parted neatly down the center of her little round head. Her black pinstriped suit was tailored to fit her small frame. And she didn't appear to have a blouse on under the jacket, not to mention the shortness of the matching skirt. She had a perfect little nose and teeth, which was nearly drowned out by the extra thick black eyeliner circling her lashes. Definitely not a picture of modesty. And definitely no light flickering in her cold dark eyes.

Then she saw him - the dark spirit named Jealousy - he was outside the window tossing around his little fiery darts. Eve immediately began to pray that he'd leave and that no dark spirits were allowed in the courtroom. Eve needed to be able to concentrate, and she knew she couldn't if Jealousy kept tossing his distracting darts at her.

It wasn't long before Hamuel appeared battle ready. His sudden appearance in the window not only made Eve flinch, but it scattered the pigeons off the outside ledge, as well as the dark spirit. Jealousy seemed more willing to retreat than do battle with Hamuel.

Eve noticed Rachel's mother enter the courtroom, the same woman she'd seen with Adam at the restaurant. But the woman who entered behind her made Eve's mouth fall open. How could it be? Was it real, or was she seeing Lisa's ghost? The young girl looked just like the picture she'd seen of Lisa Bixbee. Everything from the long dark brown hair that reached to the middle of her back, to her soft brown eyes and olive complexion, she was an identical match with Lisa.

Adam saw the look on Eve's face, so he followed her gaze and his eyes widened in surprise as well. It seemed Tracy Powers had some secrets of her own that she hadn't shared. He raised a brow to Tracy as his gaze moved back towards the judge's seat.

Rachel entered the room at the same time the jury members were brought in. Rachel's eyes were transfixed on the girl sitting directly behind Tracy Powers, Lisa's ghost.

Eve felt better knowing she wasn't the only one seeing her, so now she knew it couldn't be Lisa's ghost, but who was she?

Everyone was asked to rise as the bailiff announced the entrance of Judge Knapp, then the

Unseen

jurors were called by name, one by one, and moved to the jury box.

Bret and Paco came in together like a couple of strays. Eve noticed Rage in the hallway before the door closed behind them, but he hadn't followed them in, which must have meant her prayer was granted. She should've figured if Jealousy was rearing his evil head that Rage wouldn't be far behind.

Bret and Paco both sat on the bench against the back wall. It didn't take Bret long to notice Lisa's identical twin sister. A sister that had just popped out of the woodwork, or rather was pulled out by Tracy Powers.

Bret nudged Paco's arm. "Take a look at that, will ya."

Paco's eyes followed across the room and showed his obvious disbelief when they rested on the girl. "I yih yih. Peligro señor Bret." He muttered softly.

Bret knew the word peligro meant danger, but he didn't know why Paco would be saying it to him.

Once the twelfth and final juror was seated in the jury box, the case and docket numbers were read off for the record, along with 'State v. Rachel Ann Meade.' Then Judge Knapp requested opening statements, beginning with Tracy Powers, since she was the prosecuting attorney.

Ms. Powers stood and pulled her jacket neatly down, only to ignore the rise in her skirt, then gathered her paperwork from the table to move it to the podium. "Your honor, lady's and gentlemen of the jury. The evidence against Rachel Meade has kept her behind bars this long, lets see that it's enough to keep her there. On the night of July third, Rachel Meade was seen exiting the crime scene with the murder weapon in her hands." Tracy motioned towards the bailiff and he showed the rifle to the court, first to the judge, then the jury. "Let the Winchester M-94 Ranger rifle be entered as exhibit 'A'. Rachel's fingerprints were the only prints found on said weapon. And in matching the bullet taken from Lisa Bixbee's abdominal reign, it was proven without a doubt to be the very rifle that fired the fatal wound that ended Ms. Bixbee's life."

Tracy moved around to the front of the jury box with her hands laced together over her mid-section. The confidence in her slow stride was more than obvious. "Secondly, there are four eyewitnesses that saw Ms. Meade just moments after the incident occurred, again with the murder weapon in her hands. How much more proof do we need people? Of course she's going to deny her guilt. Who wouldn't? Even a child learns early on that lying will get them out of trouble." Waving her hand from one end of the jury box to the other, she added in closing. "Ultimately the decision rests in your hands, but keep in mind whose hands the murder weapon rested in on July third. That's all I have at this point your honor."

Tracy resumed her seat after collecting her paperwork from the podium.

Eve's fingers had a short time to rest before Adam gave his opening statement.

Adam rose to his feet when the judge looked over to him for his statement. "I realize the evidence against my client is strong, but my client had no motive. But the new evidence recently presented to me will show someone who did have motive. And once I can make contact with the EMS worker that attended Ms. Bixbee that night, he can back up my theory and reasonable motive."

Adam approached the bench with the letter in his hand. "I'd like to enter this as exhibit 'B'." He stated as he handed it up to Knapp. Then he turned back to face the jury. "This is a page from the same stationary Ms. Bixbee was writing on the night of July third. It was brought to my attention just Saturday of this week and Todd Woodrow was good enough to rush it through the forensics lab to reveal the indentations from the letter written on the previous page by Ms. Bixbee."

He paused for a moment to allow the judge time to read it over, then he continued. "The letter clearly states that Ms. Bixbee was indeed pregnant with someone's child, but she doesn't use any names."

Judge Knapp handed the letter back to Adam after having read it. "Would you please read this for the jury Mr. Webber?"

"Yes your honor." Adam retrieved the letter and read it aloud. "Darling, Soon our secret will be out. As I can only keep the evidence of our affair quiet for another seven to eight months, because you see, I'm pregnant with your child. Our child. So now would be a good time to make our love public information. I'm tired of all this sneaking around anyway. I want us to be a family someday and I want to have more children with you. I love you and I'm not ashamed to let the whole world know. I just need to know you feel the same way. Love Lisa." Adam walked over in front of the jury box. "Ladies and gentlemen, there's your motive. Whoever the darling man was, killed to keep things secret. Whether it was in a fit of rage, jealousy, or just plain violence, that, we don't know."

Adam walked back over to his table and rested his hands on both of Rachel's shoulders. Knowing the truth of Rachel's innocence gave him an added confidence as he spoke. "I ask you. Does this woman look like a ruthless killer?"

Rachel lowered her eyes away from the intent stares burning through her.

"Ms. Bixbee was not only Rachel's friend, she was her roommate. Despite any differences, that's no motive for murder." He continued on a lighter note. "Let me tell you, I had roommates so bad in college, that I'd find dirty sweaty socks being dried in the microwave, but even that wasn't worth killing for."

A soft laugh rolled through the court.

"Ms. Bixbee was still alive when my client went looking for her. Worried about her friend who hadn't yet come in from the barn. Rachel found her friend and co-worker lying in a pool of her own blood on the floor of the barn office. Imagine how devastating that must have been. Then before she could think or pick up a phone, she heard gunfire outside. In the haste of thinking the killer was still lurking around, Rachel did what anyone of us might have done to avenge our friend's attacker, she grabbed the nearest weapon. She had no way of knowing that the very rifle she chose was the very one that had been wiped down after the violent attack, and replaced like nothing ever happened. That should show you the character of this attacker. Malicious and cold hearted. To kill the woman that loved him and wanted to bear his children, and to wipe it off like dust on his boots. Why? To keep *her love* secret, how sad. He had it all, but he chose to throw it away. There was no casing found or any other evidence.

At the estimated range of the shot, Rachel should have been covered in blood, but she wasn't. The only blood found on Rachel from the victim was on the bottom of her boot. There was no way she could have cleaned up so neatly in the estimated time frame determined by forensics, which was around fifteen minutes. It would've taken her that long to run home, wash and change, then she wouldn't have time to run back to get the gun. Think about it."

Adam let go of Rachel's shoulders and moved over to his own chair. "Your honor, in light of this new evidence I would like to call a recess until I can get my key witness on the stand. I would also like to request that Ms. Bixbee's body be exhumed to verify pregnancy and a DNA test run to determine paternity."

Lisa's twin leaned forward to whisper something in Tracy's ear just before Tracy rose to her feet with her objection.

"I object your honor. This letter isn't even solid proof that it's one in the same as the deceased Lisa Bixbee. And in light of this sudden new evidence, I would like more time to prepare my case against it and this sudden key witness." Tracy's dander was in full flair as she stood behind her table.

After a moment of consideration Knapp replied. "Court will recess until tomorrow morning at nine A.M. As far as this exhumation and new evidence, I'll see you both in my chambers for a discussion. And do you have someone in mind to run the paternity test against Mr. Webber?"

"Yes I do your honor."

Diane Knapp rose to leave the room after reminding the jurors once more, not to discuss the trial with anyone, and to avoid the news in anyway – both TV, paper and above all news reporters. "Then court is recessed and I'll see you two in my chambers."

Chapter 30

"Your honor..." Tracy started out, until the judge stopped her with a raised hand.

"Please, we're in my chambers now, so feel free to call me either Ms. Knapp, or Diane. I've only been doing this a little over a year and I'm not yet used to all the formalities."

"Very well." Powers agreed. "I knew nothing of this letter until today or this surprise witness."

Adam agreed with a nod and settled back in his chair. Holding up one hand in defense he explained. "I apologize again Ms. Powers. I didn't think about the EMS worker being a witness until the proceedings were about to begin, or I would've mentioned that when I showed you the letter."

"And yet he was suddenly your *key* witness. Never the less Adam, this was all dropped on the table before me just today. With no time to prepare for any of it." Tracy chastised once more.

"It's very unethical Adam." Knapp agreed.

"I know, I've been told." He flashed a sideward glance at Tracy. "But it seems Tracy has been keeping Lisa's twin sister a secret as well."

"Well, she's not a witness in this case either." Tracy confirmed smugly. "Unless of course a character witness is needed."

"So what makes this witness a key to your case?" Knapp questioned. "And where did this sudden evidence arise from?"

Adam swallowed back the thought of ratting out Eve. His mind raced to find a way of explaining it without mentioning her name, if that was possible. "The detective told me that Ms. Bixbee had muttered something about a child to the EMS worker, so he's a witness to her final words. At the time he thought she might be in so much pain that she was delusional, since there was no child involved to his knowledge. So now there are two references to the notion that our victim was indeed pregnant."

"Okay. So once again Mr. Webber, where did this stationary page come from and how did you end up with it?" Knapp asked again.

Unseen

"A friend of mine went to Southwind looking to purchase a horse. When a business card couldn't be found, they were given this piece of stationary, since it had the ranch name, address and phone number." Adam was stalling, and from the ruffled brows on Knapp's forehead, she was losing patience with him.

"And how did this friend know to give this to you?" Knapp made quotation marks in the air as she said the word friend.

"They could tell there was indentations on the page."

"So." Knapp shrugged. "There's indentations on my stationary, but I don't expect someone to rush it off to forensics to determine what I wrote three days ago. Come on Mr. Webber, we don't have all day to pry this out of you. I want a name and I want it now. I also want to know how they knew to pass this information on to you."

Adam exhaled with a heavy heart. He asked silently for the Lord to let Eve forgive him. "Very well. Evelyn Kincaid, which answers how she knew to pass it on to me and what had happened at Southwind, and as we all know she was blind, so her sense of touch is very acute."

Diane Knapp was speechless until the shock wore off. Eve knew better, surely she had just lucked onto finding the evidence, or was her new found sight causing her to look in places better left alone? Diane saw the shock on even the bailiff's face as she looked over to ask Mr. Masters to bring Eve in the room with them.

When Matt Masters left to find Eve, the silent tension in the room grew thicker.

Adam was afraid he'd just gotten Eve canned from the trial. And Tracy seemed to simply be basking in the hot water that Adam had gotten himself into, as if applauding the punishment he was going to endure for springing last minute surprises on the court.

When Eve arrived and saw the look of regret on Adam's face, she knew the word was out without him even saying. Lifting her chin she offered Adam a curt smile to let him know it was okay.

"I'd like to speak to Ms. Kincaid alone, if you would both excuse us." Diane requested waiting until Adam and Tracy left and Eve was seated where Adam had been sitting.

Even though the mahogany leather chair was still warm from Adam's body heat, a shiver traveled the length of Eve's spine as she settled into it. She knew that Adam had no other way of explaining the stationary page without telling the judge about her, unless of course he wanted to lie, and she was much happier knowing he hadn't compromised himself in that way. Honesty was always the best way to go, in her opinion. It was also the quickest way to win her trust.

Diane listened while Eve explained herself, simply by saying, "Something just kept prompting me to go to the ranch, so I did. I wasn't intending on compromising the trial in anyway, even though I found it very hard to believe this young girl could have done such a horrendous act." Even though she knew Diane was a faith filled believer, and she could clearly see the light in her eyes, she didn't want to mention the spiritual side to her. Facts, Adam had said to stick to the facts, the physical proof.

"Because I've known you for seven years, and your aunt for twelve, I'm going to let you off easy this time. But if you so much as sigh to anyone before this trial is over, you'll be pulled from the courtroom and given a thirty-day suspension. I will, however, have to pull you as transcriber from this trial, because now you're a potential witness to validate this new evidence, and either lawyer could call you to the stand for questioning." Diane gave her a firm look. "Is that perfectly clear Ms. Kincaid?"

"Yes your honor."

The bailiff escorted her back out of the room once she agreed and she was told to remain in her office until the next case was up. Knapp instructed Matt to bring in a lunch for Eve of her choice, because she wasn't to leave the building for lunch that day. Knapp also asked the bailiff to inform Mr. Webber that a court order would be issued by the close of the day to exhume the body of Ms. Bixbee.

Chapter 31

Adam sat solemnly at his desk wishing he could've talked with Eve over lunch, but as it was, he hadn't been able to talk to her all day. He also hadn't been able to get a hold of the EMS worker, Justin Stahly, but he'd left messages at every number he had for him. A summons would be delivered to Stahly's home the following day.

Dixon and Woodrow were on their way to exhume Lisa's body. Then the body would be taken to the hospital where Woodrow could run the necessary tests immediately. So all that was left was the waiting.

Adam loathed waiting. Three years ago he had waited patiently for the jury's deliberation when a twister ripped through Wichita. Then he waited several more hours while his wife and son were dug from under the rubble of their home. They were buried in their own basement while seeking shelter from the raging F-5 tornado. Then he waited five more hours while Megan was operated on, desperately the doctors fought to save her, but their efforts were futile. His son was found dead at the scene, but he had hoped God wouldn't take his wife as well, yet he had. All his waiting had been in vain.

He shook off the thoughts of Megan and Bradley as thoughts of Eve drifted back into his mind. He had waited forty days to see if she would wake from her coma, at least that hadn't been in vain, or had it? After today she might never speak to him again. That thought had haunted him all day, especially since he couldn't even reach her by phone. If only he knew whether or not she'd be mad at him. Lying for her had crossed his mind, but he just couldn't go against his own principles, not even for her.

With so much on his mind, and a case to prepare for court in the morning, he could already see the midnight oil burning.

He tried again to regain his focus on the paperwork in front of him. He needed to prepare more questions, not only for his witnesses, but also for the prosecuting attorney's. With more witnesses and more evidence came more questions.

Unseen

He had deliberately stayed at the office to work, so his mother wouldn't disturb him by calling him up just to tell him how late it was getting. Yet he still couldn't concentrate even with all the silence in the world in his favor.

A sudden knock at the front office door jerked him quickly back to reality. He looked at the clock, noting that it was 7:15, then muttered to himself. "We're closed, can't you read? Our hours say eight to five."

"Adam, I know you're in there, your mother told me where I could find you." She called out as she knocked again.

His heart leaped at the sound of Eve's voice. His feet were aching to run to the door, but his legs were too shaky to fulfill the urge. Maybe his parents were right. This woman was already under his skin, softly burrowing her way into the very marrow of him.

Long shaky strides carried him through the door of his office, past the secretary's desk, and to the front door. He inhaled deeply to pull himself together as he unlocked the door. From the weariness on her face he could only assume she was furious with him and had come to tell him just how much.

"Please, come in and have a seat." Once Eve entered and walked past, he shut and locked the door behind her. A silent plea to God drifted through his mind as he followed her and resumed his seat.

"You've got reason enough to be angry with me, but…"

"Angry." Eve echoed out an interruption, then shamefully covered her mouth. "Sorry, I've got a bad habit of jumping in before people are done talking. But that's why I came."

"To interrupt me?"

"No." Eve giggled. She noticed Adam's posture suddenly relaxed. "And obviously it's a good thing I did, since you must have truly thought I was angry."

"I did."

"Then I'm glad I came, bearing food and forgiveness, to prove I'm not angry with you." She held up a fast food sack and assured him with a warm smile. Then she placed the sack on the desk in front of him. "In fact, this has actually shown me what an honest upright man you really are. I deserved the trouble I got myself into, and I knew I was pushing the limits, you warned me as well as my mother. I just chose not to listen to either of you, but instead I listened to the gentle whisper that kept urging me on. And if I hadn't the case wouldn't have turned in your favor. So I'm okay with being pulled as the reporter. I can still sit in on the trial and listen, since I'm now a witness to the evidence. The strange part will be when I actually have to take the stand."

Unseen

Adam felt the thousand pound weight lifting from his chest, sending a silent thank you through his mind. Here he'd been worried that she'd never speak to him again, and she not only came with forgiveness, but also to make sure he ate dinner. Her unselfish kindness was like a cool north breeze on a steamy hot summer day. No wonder he was finding himself falling head over heels for her.

"You truly are a sweetie pie." He assessed out loud as he reclined in his chair with a smile. "It's a relief to know you're forgiving instead of mad. And you can count on being called to the stand, first by me, then Powers will cross-examine you with the toughest questions and accusations she can muster."

"I know." Eve nodded and pondered the thought. From what little she knew about Ms. Powers, she knew that she would dig deep in her questioning. A warm feeling washed over her as his words echoed through her head once more, '*You truly are a sweetie pie.*' Was that a compliment or an endearment? Either way, the sound of it pleased her. "I also know that I can't discuss the case outside the courtroom any longer, so I should probably get going and not see you again until the trial is over. That way we don't raise any suspicions."

The thousand pound weight was back pressing heavy against his heart this time. He knew she was right, but he didn't have to like it. More waiting, he thought grimly. He could only hope and pray now that the trial wouldn't drag out too long. He would also do everything within his power to see that it didn't drag out long at all. He held onto the slightest bit of comfort in knowing he would at least still be able to see Eve if only briefly in the courtroom.

Eve was gone by 7:30, so Adam ate his hamburger and got back to work on the case. Worry had been replaced with a new motivation, a motivation driven by the heart. It was surprising even to Adam when he found himself done and ready to leave the office just before nine. Earlier he had anticipated being there into the wee hours of the morning. But fortunately he was wrong once more, something he was beginning to realize, wasn't always a bad thing.

Chapter 32

It was late Monday evening when Lisa's body was delivered to the hospital, but the coroner was willing to stay and open Lisa up. Upon finding the seven-week-old fetus the coroner verified pregnancy, and then he extracted what little body fluid remained in the fetus after the embalming process. They could only hope it was enough for trace to determine paternity.

DNA samples were taken from everyone at Southwind the night of the murder, but the results hadn't come back on them yet. They were expected in by Friday, which was also when Herb was expected to get back from another out of town cutting event he had went to.

Dixon made good of his time at the hospital. While he was there, he checked to see what time Justin Stahly was scheduled to work, discovering that he was on the 3 to midnight shift all week. Only at that present time Justin was out on a call, so he'd have Colby deliver the summons around eight in the morning.

With nothing left to do at the hospital, Dixon headed back to the police station, even though it was late and he should've been heading home. In route he called his wife on his cell phone to let her know he'd be home later. "I need to go over the statements I got earlier from Bret and Paco one more time." he had explained.

In his office Dixon reviewed the questions and answers from both men. In her two years working at Southwind, neither of them had ever known Lisa to have a boyfriend, or even dating anyone. Bret stated how that was frustrating to him, the fact that she was beautiful and single, but wouldn't give him or any other man the time of day. He also stated how he began to think she was gay or something. Both men agreed that they knew very little about her, and that she never spoke of herself or her past, except to say that it was all behind her where it should be.

Lisa hadn't even confided in Rachel by mentioning her past. So from all Dixon had gathered so far, no one at Southwind knew Lisa had a twin, or any other living family members for that matter. Herb had been the one to hire Lisa, and since he was out of town, Dixon hadn't yet been able to find out if he even knew about this twin sister.

Talking with Tracy Powers, Dixon found out that the mysterious twin's name was Felicia and how she found her, which had been from a two-year-old letter found in Lisa's things. Fortunately Powers was able to still reach Felicia at the same address, since she was still living there and attending college in Wichita. There was grandparents mentioned in the letter, but Powers was unable to track them down, since Felicia wasn't willing to share that information. She did, however, share the fact that their father ran out on them when they were seven, and their mother died when they were seventeen, so their grandparents took them in for a few years after that.

From what Powers had gathered from Felicia, Lisa had seemingly dropped off the face of the earth two years ago. That was when Felicia had lost contact with her sister and she was never sure why. Felicia didn't know Lisa was even in Dodge City, little alone where she was working, until receiving the letter from Powers about Lisa's death.

Colby Daubs peered through Dixon's door. "We both seem to be putting in a long day. What's your excuse? Mine is because I'm still trying to keep from dwelling on Mandy's death, but working on a murder case seems to only be making it worse. I've been praying and going to church like I need to, but it just hasn't seemed to help."

"I can imagine. I'm just wondering if we're going to be able to pinpoint who this mysterious man is that Lisa was having an affair with." George hadn't gone to church himself in years, although his wife was still faithful about going, so he was afraid to make any comments regarding church at that point in time.

Colby entered the room and took the seat on the other side of Dixon's desk. "Yah, it seems this girl was all too good at keeping secrets, even from her own twin. And I've always heard that identical twins are closer than regular sisters."

"Apparently not these two." Dixon lifted an envelope. "Here's the summons for Stahly. It'll be right here on my desk in the morning, so as soon as you get here I'd like you to run it by his place."

"Sure thing. And what time does court begin?"

"At nine."

"So do you still think Rachel's the killer, or some guy?"

Dixon took a deep breath of uncertainty. "Well, it sounds like the guy had a motive, if only to silence her. And the missing pillow wouldn't be enough to stop any blood spatter from getting on Rachel, so

I don't think she would've had time to pull it off. I knew things weren't adding up, we just didn't have any other leads until this letter showed up."

"Yah. So I guess it was truly a God thing that Eve risked everything by going to the ranch and finding it."

"News travels fast around here doesn't it?"

Colby nodded an agreement. "Especially something like this. Getting pulled from the case, risking her job. I'm just glad Knapp went that easy on her."

Dixon checked the time. "Speaking of risks, I'll be risking my own neck if I don't get home pretty soon."

"Yah, I'd better get out of here too."

They walked out together in silence. Both were still undoubtedly rolling over the case in their minds. There was a killer in Dodge City that needed to meet the long arm of the law.

Chapter 33

Tuesday morning the trial resumed and Paco was the first witness called to the stand by Ms. Powers. Maggy had been called in to transcribe the trial, so for the first time ever, Eve had to simply sit, listen and pray. And pray she did when she saw Rage and Jealousy starting to enter the courtroom along with another dark spirit that she didn't know.

Once Paco was sworn in and seated, Tracy gathered her papers and stood up behind the podium. "Mr. De la Puente would you tell the court what you were doing on the night of July 3rd between eleven and midnight?" Tracy started out.

"I went to bed at ten thirty after the news was over." He replied in his heavy Spanish accent.

"What woke you up and sent you outside with a rifle?"

"I heard something, but I wasn't sure what it was, so I sat up to listen. After a few minutes I heard the mares fussing, so I throw on some clothes to go check it out."

Tracy tapped her pen on the pulpit a few times before going on to her next question. "What made you grab your rifle as you went out to check on the mares?"

Paco shrugged. "Because I knew the foals were out with the mares and we've had trouble in the past with the coyotes getting our foals."

"So then the only noise you heard were the horses, is that correct?"

"The only noise I can remember, yes."

"So after you fired a shot in the air to scare off the coyotes, is that when you saw Rachel run out of the barn with a rifle in her hands?"

Paco nodded out his response and the judge was quick to remind him that he needed to make a verbal response for the court reporter, so he in turn did so.

"Did she run towards you in a panic, or with the weapon raised as if to attack you?"

Paco's brow creased in thought as he tried hard to remember. "I think it was at her side."

"So then did she shoot at the coyotes herself when she reached you, Mr. De la Puente?" She continued after he stated that Rachel hadn't fired the rifle to his knowledge. "Who was the next person to see Rachel with the gun?"

"First my sister Lolita, then señor Bret, and finally señor Herb."

"Did Rachel act strange in anyway?"

Paco took a moment to think. "She was worked up, but I thought it was because of my shot and the coyotes."

"Is that because Rachel had said nothing about Ms. Bixbee being shot and lying in a pool of her own blood?" Paco said yes, so Tracy quickly jumped to the next question. "How long did it take Rachel to say anything about Ms. Bixbee?"

"I'm not sure, maybe about ten minutes."

"And why do you suppose she mentioned her at that time?"

"Objection your honor that's speculation." Adam raised a motion against the question.

"Sustained." Knapp ruled and the question was withdrawn.

"Then let me rephrase your honor. How did Rachel bring up the subject?"

"Señor Herb made a statement about all of us being drawn out of bed except Lisa, that's when

Rachel told us it was because Lisa had been shot and we need to call an ambulance."

"So there was at least a ten minute lapse between the time she came running out, to the time she stated that someone needed to call an ambulance?"

"Objection, that's more speculation."

"Sustained." Knapp ruled again.

Tracy let out a heavy breath to another withdrawn question, especially since she felt that it needed to stand. Yet she plunged on to her next question. She asked about the relationship between Rachel and Lisa, if there were ever any harsh words or threats thrown around between the two. None that Paco had ever known about, but he did say that the two girls had a lot of competition between them, always trying to see which one of them was the best at this or that. Paco also stated how one day they were like best friends and the next they might barely speak to one another. When Tracy was done she sat back down to let Adam cross examine the witness.

"Considering the confusion of finding her friend shot and hearing your gun fire, then three other people show up one after the other, that's a lot to happen in a short time. Is it possible señor De la Puente, that Rachel just didn't get an opportunity to mention Lisa's condition right away?" Adam began his questioning around the time frame issue.

"I suppose señor."

"And did you notice any blood on Ms. Meade?"

"No señor."

"But yet you saw her running out of the barn and not from her trailer?"

"That's right."

"So if she had just shot Lisa, at the estimated range of three feet, she should've had blood splattered on her somewhere, wouldn't you agree?"

"Yes."

"She couldn't have changed if you saw her exiting the barn. There was no time or place, besides a water hose, for her to clean up. Furthermore, if she had just shot someone, why would she run straight towards the nearest witness with the murder weapon in tow? So then wouldn't it only make sense to say that she did indeed enter the barn *after* Ms. Bixbee had already been shot?" Adam's gaze moved over the jury before returning to Paco with his hands lifted out in question.

"I don't guess she would. Unless she was disoriented or perhaps it was an accident."

"But why wasn't there any blood on her?"

"I don't know señor Webber. She could have had a rain slicker on."

"The barn was searched and nothing like that was found. No discarded bullet casing. No blood spattered clothing. No pillow from the office couch. Yet all those things should have been somewhere. So someone was there before Ms. Meade. Someone who had the time to hide or discard any and all evidence pointing the finger at them. Can your sister verify that you were indeed in bed sleeping?"

"Yes, she lives with me, and she was there when I went to my room. A few minutes later I heard her go to her room." Paco's brow showed his frustration at the turn of questioning, since it was once more pointing a finger towards him.

So far Eve's praying had kept the dark spirits out of the courtroom, but at Paco's rising frustration she noticed another unfamiliar spirit peeking through the window at her. She suspected there were a lot of dark spirits lurking around outside the windows, since she hadn't heard the usual coo of the pigeons that often perched on the ledges. Hamuel, Adam's angel Abijah and Rachel's angel Halohesh were the only spirits in the courtroom. And Rachel's angel was the only one moving around, whispering something to every one of the jury members, one at a time.

"So were you listening for her to go to bed so that you could get up once she was asleep?"

"Objection your honor, he's badgering the witness." Powers blurted without hesitation.

"Do you have a point to make with this question Mr. Webber?" The judge asked.

"Yes, I do your honor."

"Then I suggest you hurry up and make your point without badgering Mr. Webber. Go ahead and answer the question Mr. De la Puente."

"No, I wasn't." Paco scowled.

"And did anyone else see the coyotes you were shooting at señor De la Puente?"

Paco's scowl deepened. Now he knew were the questions were heading and he didn't like it one bit, since Adam was indeed turning the finger on him. "I don't know señor. Rachel may have seen them but I think they were gone by the time everyone else came out."

"So then the question arises as to whether or not there really were any coyotes at all. Is it possible that you were merely staging a show to cover up the sounds from the first gun fire, or to raise a confusion to draw everyone out in hopes that they would discover the body before morning?"

"Objection your honor Mr. De la Puente is not charged with this crime."

"Sustained." The judge had to agree. "What is the point you were aiming for Mr. Webber?"

"Paco could have killed Ms. Bixbee and then caused the confusion to throw the suspicion off himself. So my point is, your honor, that anyone at the ranch that night could have committed this crime, and that Paco had no more motive than my client for wanting Ms. Bixbee dead. Unless of course it turns out that Lisa was indeed pregnant and that Paco is the child's father."

"And when will the DNA results be back on that Mr. Webber?" Knapp questioned.

"I'm hoping by this Friday your honor." Adam made a quick scan over his notes. "I have no further questions your honor."

Knapp glanced over at Powers who answered silently with a head shake that she had nothing further either, so the judge told Paco he could step down from the stand, and court was recessed until after lunch.

Adam wanted to go to lunch with Eve, but he had to respect her wishes, first of all because she was right and secondly because he did respect her. So he had to refrain from seeing her too much until after the trial was over. Which would be his motivation to make sure it was a swift just trial. Although when she past him in the hallway, and spoke, he couldn't resist the urge to respond back to her.

"It's Bret not Paco." Eve muttered, just barely loud enough for him to hear.

"I know." Adam mumbled back in an equally low voice. He also knew if he could raise any doubt at all, in even one juror's mind then they couldn't find Rachel guilty beyond all reasonable doubt.

Chapter 34

After lunch Lolita was called to the stand. She was sworn in and seated, then questioned by Tracy Powers. Most of the prosecuting attorney's questions to Lolita were the same general type questions she'd asked Paco. It was clear from her questioning that she didn't have as many years of experience as Adam did.

Adam had his own plans. He wanted to redirect the focus from Rachel and onto the father of Lisa's unborn child. Woodrow was in the courtroom, so Adam was anxious to find out if the first DNA tests were back. It was going to take at least another week to get back the DNA test on the fetus, even though it was sent in as a rush job, so they were still nearly two weeks away from proving whether or not Bret was the father.

Adam stood and walked around in front of his table to cross-examine the witness. "Señorita De la Puente, on the night Lisa Bixbee was shot, did you or did you not see the coyotes your brother had shot at?"

"No señor, I didn't."

"So then you cannot be one hundred percent sure there actually were any coyotes, can you?" He crossed his arms over his chest waiting for her answer. He noted the cringed looked she flashed at Paco just before answering the question. He hoped there were a few jury members that noticed that look as well.

"No, but my brother wouldn't lie about it."

"So your brother has never lied, not even once in his entire life? Remember Ms. De la Puente, you are under oath, and it's perjury if you don't tell the truth."

"Hasn't everyone lied at one time or another?"

"Just answer yes or no please." Adam wasn't going to let her slide by answering a question with a question.

"Yes, he has lied before." She replied softly with her head lowered, as if she knew she was setting her brother up for a fall.

"Louder please so that all the jury members can hear you." Knapp reminded her.

Lolita repeated her answer louder.

"And how long have you known the defendant, Rachel Meade?"

"For about seven years, since she came to work for señor Louis."

Adam walked back around behind the table to look at his notes. "And you've worked for Mr. Louis for about ten, is that correct?"

"Yes."

"In that time have you ever known Rachel to lie to you?"

Lolita closed her dark eyes to think for a moment. "I've never caught her lying, but…"

"Answer yes or no please." Adam reminded her.

She took a deep breath before answering. "No señor."

"It's also my understanding that you do the laundry at Southwind." He went on after she replied with a simple yes. "Do you also wash your brother's clothes, or anyone else's at the ranch?"

"Objection your honor, I don't see what relevance these questions have to the case." Powers interjected.

"Overruled. Get to your point quickly Mr. Webber." Knapp looked back to the witness. "You may answer the question, yes or no."

"Yes." Lolita answered with some reservation.

"After Lisa's death, did you ever notice blood on anyone's clothing or any clothing missing?"

"I notice no blood. I do so much laundry that I don't notice something missing, with six people there's just too much to keep track of."

"Did Lisa ever make your brother angry?"

Lolita hesitated again and gave her brother an apologetic look. "I think she made everyone angry with her at one time or another."

"So even you have gotten mad at her then, is that correct?"

"Yes."

"And why did you get mad at her Ms. De la Puente?"

"She didn't like me folding a shirt she wanted hung up, so I told her she could do her own laundry then. She was very particular that way. Everything had to be just so so." Lolita made quotation marks in the air with her fingers at the words 'so so.'

"Has Paco, to your knowledge, ever threatened either Lisa or Rachel in anyway?"

"One time Lisa made him angry and he threatened to get her fired, but he never threatened to kill her, or anybody else."

By the time Adam had finished with Lolita, he felt confident that the jury would be wondering if Paco killed Lisa Bixbee. He had time, possible motive and even a possible distraction to place him away from the scene long enough for someone else to notice the body.

Once court was recessed until the following day, Adam quickly caught up with Todd Woodrow and Dixon at the police station. He immediately asked if the results of the DNA were in. He was glad to hear that the results on Bret and Paco had just been faxed over.

"We still need to get back the results from Herb's DNA." Todd reminded.

"Herb?" Adam echoed. "Do you really suppose it could be Herb?" He went on after Todd shrugged out a reply. "I guess it would make sense. He'd want to keep their affair silent; after all, the guy is nearly thirty years older than Lisa was. Plus he's already had one wife and son leave him, which I heard had something to do with another man, but I never really bought that bit of gossip. No, it couldn't be." Adam shook off the idea. "I'm as sure as I am sitting here that Bret's the father."

"Herb won't be back to take the stand 'til Friday," Dixon added his voice into the conversation. "and this is just Tuesday. Do you think you can keep this trial going until Herb gets back?"

"Bret will be called to the stand tomorrow, so if I can keep him there all day I might be able to drag it out until Thursday. Then there's still the two of you to call to the stand along with Justin Stahly, plus now Eve can be called to the stand. So I'm sure I'll be able to stall until we get Herb on the stand." Adam concurred. Another thought brought a sudden frown to his brow. "But then we'll still have to wait another week for the DNA results on the fetus." Adam rubbed his head as another thought hit him. "If Bret, or even if Herb turns out to be the child's father, why would Lisa have to write a letter to tell him? Why couldn't she simply walk up to the main house to tell him?"

"Maybe that was all part of keeping things secret." Dixon quickly summed up.

The three men discussed the case a few more hours before Adam left Dixon's office. All the while Adam kept wanting to talk to Eve.

He respected her wishes to tone things down until the trial was over, but she was now *his* witness on the stationary page. That meant he could see her or talk to her about the case whenever he needed to. The thought of it brought him a strange tingle of joy that he didn't understand. Adam did need to talk to Eve about the second vision she had, in hopes of finding out if it had possibly been Herb that she saw.

"Too bad we couldn't get them all in for a line-up and have them turn their backs to Eve so she could identify the killer." Adam muttered to himself then turned on the radio in his jeep to get his mind on something relaxing.

That night when Adam got home he called Eve and asked her again if she got any other view of the killer besides the back of his head. Eve told him that she hadn't, and that the only other thing she might have to identify the killer was the cologne she remembered smelling in the vision. She had thought it was a fluke that she could smell things in the first vision until it happened again with the second one. Plus she had never seen or met Herb before, so she had no idea what he even looked like. That's when Adam told her that they both had black hair and were about the same build, and that Herb was only four inches taller.

Chapter 35

At nine thirty Wednesday morning Bret was called to the witness stand.

Eve sat in the back row next to the window listening as Tracy Powers began her questioning. Eve found the soft cooing of a pigeon just outside the window soothing to her restless nerves, especially since she had come to know that the absence of cooing meant the presence of evil.

"So Mr. Louis would you describe for the court Rachel's state of mind when you first ran outside to see what the commotion was all about?" Powers lightly tapped her pen on the podium as she waited for his answer.

"I guess she was anxious and excited like everyone else." Bret answered as he looked directly at Rachel.

"Was she crying, upset, or in any other way grieved about finding Lisa shot?"

"Her eyes misted up a little when she told us what she saw and that someone needed to call an ambulance." He stated to the best of his knowledge.

"What did she do after telling you about Lisa?"

"That's when we all ran to the barn and saw Lisa lyin' there. I called 911 while Rachel tried to stop the bleeding by holding pressure on the wound."

"So at this point you were all in the barn office, is that correct?"

"Yah." Bret said briefly.

"And was Lisa still alive at that time?"

Bret nodded his head as he gave a verbal reply. "Yah, but she was unconscious."

"With two people holding rifles, who were you more inclined to suspect as the shooter at that point?"

"Objection, that's speculation." Adam voiced out.

"Overruled." Knapp denied. "Answer the question please Mr. Louis."

"I honestly had suspicions about both of them."

"Have you ever known Lisa and Rachel to argue or fight over things in the past?"

"I've heard them argue a few times about getting things done around the place. Lisa was not only a perfectionist she was a little on the bossy side, and sometimes that made Rachel mad, since Rachel had worked there longer and had more experience."

"Have you ever heard Rachel threaten the victim before?" Tracy tucked her hair behind her right ear.

"No, but I've heard Lisa threaten to get Rachel fired a few times."

Tracy asked a few more questions dealing with the events that unfolded the night Lisa was shot. Like what everyone was wearing. Bret remembered that both he and Herb only took time to slide on their jeans, and Lolita had on a robe, so Rachel and Paco had been the only two fully dressed. Once Tracy was done questioning Bret, she gathered her notes and gave the floor over to Adam.

"So both you and your father were in bed when you heard the shot fired, is that correct?" Adam started out as he stood up behind the table.

"That's correct."

"And you can both vouch for one another?"

"Yah."

"Did you both go up to your rooms at the same time?"

Bret shook his head as he answered. "No, dad went up first, then I went up about thirty minutes later."

"Then your father didn't actually see you go into your room, is that correct?"

"That's correct." Bret agreed again.

"Is it true, that in the past two years since Lisa has worked for your father, that you continuously pursued and were continuously rejected by the victim?"

"You sure don't hesitate to get too personal do you?" Bret scoffed.

"A murder trial is *very* personal Mr. Louis, so please just answer yes or no."

"Yah. But that doesn't make me a lady killer just because I love the ladies." Bret smirked at his own smug humor.

Adam raised a brow at Bret's jovial attitude. "Did you also find it funny when Lisa cringed in pain while you were biting her neck?"

"What?" Bret bellowed out as if he had no idea.

"We got back the DNA results today and we know for sure that the teeth bruising left in Ms. Bixbee's neck came from you. There was not only traces of your saliva still lingering on her skin, but from the teeth pattern it clearly shows a gap between the two front teeth that is consistent with your own bite pattern. You see, teeth prints are about as unique as finger prints." Adam held out a hand toward Bret. "Would you care to deny it now Mr. Louis?"

"No, but a bite mark doesn't mean that I killed her or would even want to kill her." Bret stated on a more serious note.

"Perhaps not. But rejection after rejection could easily set off a man with a tempter like yours."

"Objection your honor that's speculation." Powers voiced out.

"Do you know his temperament for a fact Mr. Webber?" Knapp questioned.

"Yes I do your honor and I have personally witnessed one of his outrages." Adam assured the judge.

"Overruled. You may answer the question Mr. Louis." The judge ordered.

Tracy huffed out her disappointment at the ruling.

"Tell the court then Mr. Louis what caused you to bite Lisa on the neck that day?"

"I was just playin' around with her. Nothing more."

"Seems like pretty rough play when it causes bruising. Perhaps you were making love to the victim when this bite occurred and you just got carried away in the heat of passion. Is that what happened Mr. Louis?"

Bret burst into laughter. "Not hardly Mr. Webber." He spit out Adam's name as if it were a bad taste in his mouth. "You said it yourself, I tried but I was always rejected."

"Then perhaps you forced yourself on her and when she threatened to tell your father you shot her to keep her quiet. Or perhaps it angered you when you found out she was pregnant. Was it your child she was carrying Mr. Louis?"

"Objection, this witness hasn't been charged with this crime."

"Overruled. Answer the question please."

"My child? I didn't even know she was pregnant, but I do know it wasn't mine because I never touched her." Bret barked.

"Yet you felt an overwhelming desire to bite her neck until it was bruised?"

Bret's anger was rising, literally rising from out of the floor behind him, as Rage began creeping up out of the floor in Bret's shadow. Rage had to avoid Eve's eyes, so she wouldn't see him and stop him before he accomplished his task.

Adam's questions prodded at Bret like a hot branding iron raising Bret's temper with every question. Tracy called out a few objections, but the judge overruled them all. With all the rising frustration from Bret, and even Tracy, Rage grew stronger as he worked his way through the floor.

Eve suddenly realized she had stopped praying to listen to Adam's interrogation go on. She also noticed the cooing outside the window had stopped.

Then suddenly Rage sprang up behind Bret, as Bret's face burned red with anger. He was furious with Adam's accusations, and it clearly showed. The dark spirit buried his fingers into Bret's head while hissing out obscenities, that luckily only Eve could hear, yet things she wished she couldn't hear. Things about her and how it was all her fault and that she should be taught a lesson for snooping into things that didn't concern her.

When Bret's eyes turned their focus onto Eve, she swallowed back the lump in her throat and began to pray under her breath.

"*S-S-Stop it.*" Rage hissed out looking directly at Eve. "*Shut up. You don't know what you're saying. Your prayers are weak. You feeble human.*"

Eve prayed harder and louder, but not loud enough for anyone else to hear her.

Rage released his hold on Bret's mind to cover his own ears with his hands. He was trying to blot out Eve's words from his mind. "*S-S-Stop it.*" He hissed again. "*No more. I don't want to hear anymore from you.*"

Eve wasn't about to stop until she saw Hamuel, who came as quickly as her next breath, and he snatched Rage up by one arm and swiftly removed him from the courtroom.

That was when Eve noticed there was another dark spirit that had been lurking in the shadow of Rage's image. This was a dark spirit that Eve hadn't seen before. In his bony gray hand he was holding a tarnished silver chalice. Eve's prayer ceased for only a moment as she watched the dark spirit tip the cup up over Bret's head. He poured a dark liquid out over Bret, and immediately Eve could see the look of hatred enter into Bret's darkened eyes as they narrowed on her.

She wanted to run from the courtroom, but then she remembered what Hamuel had told her about not having a spirit of fear. That's when she closed her eyes to everything around her, focusing on her prayer and the one she was praying to. She didn't open her eyes until she heard the crashing of swords outside end. When she did look up she saw Adam's angel removing the second dark spirit from the courtroom.

It was a relief when Eve heard the judge call a recess for lunch and that court would resume the following day instead of after lunch. Due to the fact that Adam had requested a continuance, since his key witness, Justin Stahly, was unable to be in court until Thursday.

Chapter 36

Thursday morning the questioning started out with Dixon taking the stand. Dixon explained how he had been called out from home to work the scene at Southwind, because the night shift detective was already out on the DUI accident involving Mandy Daubs. He also told the court what he found when he investigated the crime scene, which hadn't been too much at all, since most of the evidence had already been removed.

After Powers cross-examined Dixon, Woodrow was called to the stand. He gave his theory of a pillow being used to muffle the sound of the shot. Which also gave an explanation as to why no one had heard another shot before the one Paco fired off into the air.

"And what evidence is there to back up your theory Mr. Woodrow?" Adam asked as he leaned back against his table and crossed his ankles together in a relaxed manor.

"There were white polyester fibers found on the body and at the scene that are consistent with those used to stuff pillows." Todd responded. "Plus everyone at the ranch will attest to the fact that there was a throw pillow on the office sofa that is now missing."

"Is there any other evidence that points to my client being the killer beside her finger prints on the rifle? Was the pillow, bloody clothing, or anything else found when Ms. Meade's trailer was searched?"

"No."

Adam asked a few more questions about the estimated distance of the shot and how many blood spatters there would have been from a rifle shot at such close range. Woodrow concluded that even with the pillow being used to muffle the sound there would have been a substantial amount of spatter in both directions from the entry wound. So there would have been no way the shooter could have left the scene without trace amounts of blood on them.

Tracy's cross-examination was a desperate attempt to gain back the ground she knew she'd lost. Yet there was nothing else on Rachel to pin her with the murder of Lisa Bixbee, she knew it, and the jury knew it. She could already feel the trial turning in Rachel's favor even though they still hadn't heard from Herb or Justin. And Tracy was pushing to get Rachel herself called to the stand, even though Adam had been trying to derail her efforts, just as he was trying to keep Eve from being called to the stand.

After lunch Justin was finally put on the stand. He told the court how Lisa had gained consciousness twice during the ride to the hospital.

"And did Ms. Bixbee say anything during those brief moments of consciousness?" Adam questioned.

"Yes."

"And what did she say Mr. Stahly?"

"It was a little hard to hear her, since she had an oxygen mask over her face, but I heard some of it. The first time Lisa spoke, she asked, 'Did he hurt my baby?' And the second time she said, 'Please don't let me die. I can't die yet.' She mumbled some more after that but I couldn't understand what it was. By then the meds were really starting to kick in and making her groggy." Justin explained.

"But you clearly heard Lisa say *he*. 'Did *he* hurt my baby?" Adam asked once more to raise the issue to the jury.

"That's correct."

"So then did you ask her where her baby was?"

Justin rubbed his chin with his thumb and forefinger as he thought back to that night. "I think I did, since I hadn't seen or heard anything prior to that about a baby being involved in any way. But she didn't respond, so that's when I figured she was delusional from the pain and the meds, and that she probably didn't even know what she was saying."

"And why didn't the hospital run a pregnancy test on her?" Adam inquired.

"That's not like standard procedure or anything. They simply determine cause of death, unless there's an issue raised for something else to be done. However, if she had been far enough along to be showing signs of pregnancy, they would have checked to see if the fetus was still alive."

Adam finished with the witness and let Tracy have to floor for cross-examination.

"So Mr. Stahly, how is it that you could clearly hear the victim say 'Did he hurt my baby' yet other words were too mumbled to hear?"

"She didn't always speak loud enough to hear her through the mask and over the siren."

"Then how can you be sure she in fact said he? Isn't it just as likely that she could have said she?" Tracy raised her brows as she looked over at the jury.

Justin gave the question a little thought before answering. "No, I specifically remember her saying he."

"But if you thought she was delusional. Then how can we be sure she knew what she was saying? Perhaps she hadn't meant to say he at all."

"At that point I wasn't too sure, but now that I know there was indeed a baby involved, I'm sure she knew what she was saying and that I was wrong to think she was delusional."

Tracy's questioning began showing her desperation, since she felt even more ground slipping away underneath her. From the testimonies given, even she was beginning to wonder if Rachel was innocent, so she knew a doubt had to be rising in the minds of the jury.

Adam called out a few objections when Tracy began badgering his witness. Judge Knapp not only sustained the majority of Adam's objections, but she ended up calling a recess until the following day, at which point Herb, Rachel or Eve would be called to take the stand.

Chapter 37

After court Adam took time to talk with both Rachel and Eve. He had to prepare them in case they had to take the stand. He wanted to keep Rachel from going to the stand, but she wanted the court to hear her out, so she convinced Adam to let her testify. Eve wasn't afraid of approaching the stand either, since she knew the jury needed to be assured of where the stationary page came from, especially since it had been the turning point in the issue of another suspects' possible motive and involvement.

So when Friday morning arrived, Eve was prayed up and she had even fasted breakfast that morning just to empower her spirit over the dark spirits that she knew would be trying to intimidate her testimony. She had suggested for Rachel to do the same, only she wasn't sure she had followed her advice.

Eve was the first called to the stand.

"So Ms. Kincaid, what prompted you to go to Southwind in the first place?" Adam began the questioning.

"Since learning how to ride horses I've discovered that I enjoy riding very much, so I was looking into the cost of purchasing one of my own."

"And why did you choose Southwind?"

"Because I'd heard they breed and sell horses."

"So do I, yet you never came to me looking to buy a horse."

Eve swallowed back her own surprise at his unexpected question. It wasn't one of the questions they had discussed in yesterdays meeting. "I didn't realize that at the time."

The left side of Adam's lips curled ever so slightly at his pleasure in her answer, since it was exactly what he'd expected her to say. He knew it wasn't a question he'd rehearsed with her yesterday, but he knew it was on Bret's mind, and possibly the jury's as well. "Tell the court then how it was that you ended up with this stationary page."

"Bret Louis couldn't find a business card anywhere in the desk, so he lifted up the desk top calendar and pulled out a stationary tablet with the ranch name, address and phone number on it for me." Eve explained detailing the steps Bret made that afternoon.

Adam raised a brow of interest, since she hadn't told him before where exactly it was Bret had gotten the tablet. "Under the desk top calendar you say?"

"That's correct."

"So he knew exactly where the tablet was, yet he didn't know exactly where the business cards were. Hum." Adam looked over to the jury as he rubbed his chin. "I find that very interesting. Most people, especially men, don't tend to look under anything to find anything. I know I've been accused of it more than once."

A soft laughter came from the jury at his comment.

"Then explain to the court why you thought to bring this page to the authorities."

"I knew a little about the case, since I transcribed the preliminary hearing. And since I used to be blind my sense of touch is still very acute, so once I realized Lisa's signature was indented in the paper, I thought it might have some significance. Only I didn't realize how much until after the page was processed by forensics."

"How could you be sure it was one in the same Lisa as our victim? Seeing that she didn't sign a last name."

"Because I knew it came from the very ranch Lisa had worked at."

Adam looked up at the judge and concluded that he had no further questions. He smiled slightly again when Powers declined to cross-examine Eve. It not only played in Rachel's favor, but it meant she had no way of disputing the escalating idea of a male suspect, which was beginning to look more and more like Bret all the time.

Next Rachel was called to the stand and sworn in.

"Ms. Meade, what was it that woke you and sent you out to the barn the night Lisa was killed?" Adam stood and began his questioning from behind his table.

"I heard something."

"A shot perhaps?"

"I wasn't sure. I thought it was more like one of the horses kicking at the stall." Rachel clarified.

"Is that what prompted you to look out your window?"

"Yes."

"Did you see anyone at that point?"

"No, but I noticed the barn light was still on and that Lisa had been the last one out there."

Adam paced around to the front of the table and leaned back on it, like he so often did. "Do you know why Lisa was the last one in the barn that night?"

"Yes."

"And why was that Ms. Meade?"

"She said she had to write a letter."

"Did she tell you who the letter was too?"

"No, and I knew better than to pry, since she didn't like that."

"So then what did you do?" Adam crossed his arms over his chest.

"First I went to her room to tell her that she didn't get the light shut off, but she didn't answer, so I peeked in. When I saw her bed was still made I knew she had to still be in the barn, so I went out to make sure she was all right."

"And what time did all this take place?"

"It was twelve A.M. when I looked at the clock."

"And what time had it been when you left her in the barn?"

"About ten."

"So there was two hours between the last time you saw her alive to the time you found her shot." Adam said it as a statement more for the jury to hear than for Rachel to answer. "That gave someone two full hours to get in and out of the barn, shoot Lisa and hide all evidence. Did police find any blood evidence in your home indicating you had went home, cleaned up, and then went back later to reclaim the murder weapon?"

"No."

"Oddly enough, they found no evidence anywhere that anyone had cleaned blood off of them in or around the barn. It's just as if all other evidence of this crime got up and walked away. Unless whoever shot Lisa went out behind the house to the creek to wash all the evidence down stream." The thought sent a shiver up Adam's spine, since his parent's pond was down stream of Southwind. "Since the victim was estimated to have been shot between eleven and eleven thirty P.M., that would have given you an hour to get to the creek, wash away the blood and dispose of evidence. But the question remains, why would you leave the rifle with your fingerprints all over it?"

"I wouldn't." Rachel admitted. "Not if I had done something wrong with it, but since I hadn't, I had no idea that it had been used to shoot Lisa."

Adam asked a few more questions before turning things over to Tracy. But he felt confident that he had shown the jury the irrational suggestion that Rachel could have, or would have killed Lisa.

Tracy stepped up to the podium with her notes in tow. "Ms. Meade, we already know from the testimonies of others that you and Lisa had an unspoken type of rivalry, is that correct?"

"We challenged each other if that's what you mean." Rachel shifted in her seat.

"So then, how might you react if you were to find out that Lisa was pregnant with your boyfriends' child?" Tracy slung out the unexpected question as if it were a boomerang.

"I'd be deeply hurt, but I wouldn't kill her or my boyfriend for that matter. No one is worth killing for. In fact I might even be relieved to know about his infidelities before he became my husband."

'*Good for you.*' Eve thought to herself.

"Yet people have been known to kill over infidelities and jealousy's." Tracy reminded with a stern glare.

"Maybe, but that doesn't mean all people react that way Ms. Powers." Rachel reminded her with an equally stern look.

"Did you know about Lisa's pregnancy before she was killed?"

"No, I didn't."

"Did you know Lisa had a twin sister named Felicia? Or any other family members for that matter?" Powers walked back to her table to collect some more information while she waited for the defendant's response.

"No I didn't. For some reason she didn't like people prying into her private life, so the few times I asked her any personal questions, she told me that they were all in her past and that's where she wanted them to stay. She seemed to like the air of mystery around her that way."

"You say you left the victim alone in the barn around ten thirty."

"That's correct."

"What's to say you didn't leave later, like more around eleven, shooting her before you left. Only to realized later that you forgot to remove your fingerprints from the murder weapon. Isn't that why you went back out to the barn Ms. Meade, was to remove the rifle and dispose of it in the same place you hid everything else?"

"No, that's not true." Rachel's smooth tan brow creased with a frown.

"What you didn't count on was getting stopped by Paco who was merely protecting the foals. Isn't that right?"

"No, you're wrong." Rachel's frown deepened.

"I think you were attempting to dispose of the gun when Paco unexpectedly came out and boggled your plans."

"Objection your honor, she's badgering the witness."

"Sustained. Save your accusations for the closing statement Ms. Powers. Focus on questioning the witness if you would please."

"Sorry your honor." Tracy backed down and finished up with her last few questions. "Did you see the coyotes that Paco was shooting at when you ran out from the barn?"

Unseen

"No."

"Then why did you come running out with the rifle in your hands?"

"Because I thought that whoever shot Lisa was still around shooting at someone else."

"So was your intent to be the hero by saving the next possible victim? Like some sort of super hero saving the day?"

A soft laughter came from a few of the jury members.

"Not to be a hero, but I did hope to stop the shooter from shooting anyone else."

When Tracy concluded that she had no further questions, Knapp called for a recess until after lunch.

Chapter 38

*H*erb arrived home around ten A.M. and was on the witness stand by one, directly after lunch. Tracy was the first one to question the witness. She started off by asking Herb what had drawn him outside; he answered that it was the gunshot he heard. His testimony was in basic agreement with everyone else's, so Tracy's questions didn't draw out any new information for the jury.

However, when Adam cross-examined Herb, he brought out a few excellent points that neither he nor the jury knew before that point. Especially when he asked, "Did you by any chance know that Ms. Bixbee was pregnant?"

"Yes, I did." Herb responded.

Adam was taken with surprise to hear that he knew. "When and how did you find this out Mr. Louis?"

"Lisa told me about two weeks before she was shot."

"And why do you suppose she told you? Was it simply because you were her employer?"

"No." Herb cleared his throat before explaining. "It was because she tried to tell me it was mine."

Adam raised a brow at Herb's willingness to confess. "And was it your child?"

"No."

"And how can you be so sure of that Mr. Louis?"

"Because right after she told me we went to the hospital and had a paternity test done." Herb admitted.

Bret's chin dropped, leaving his mouth wide open from the shock. Paco shrugged when Bret glanced over at him, since this was all news to him as well. No one would have ever guessed Lisa was messing around with Herb.

Dixon quickly took out a notebook from his pocket to jot down an address if Adam asked the next question he was sure he'd ask.

"What hospital was that Mr. Louis?" Adam asked it just as Dixon had assumed he would.

"St. Joseph in Wichita. We were there at a cutting horse event that was going on at the coliseum. I remember that specifically, because I paid extra for them to put a rush on the test. I wanted to know the truth before we got back home, but I found out it wasn't mine, that's when I ended the relationship with her. I also told her she had one month to find another job and leave my property."

Dixon indeed jotted down the hospital to verify Herb's story and to have the information Faxed over. He leaned over and whispered to Woodrow. "Now we may not have to wait on the DNA results of the fetus." Then the two of them quietly slipped out of the courtroom to see if they could get that information before Herb was even off the witness stand.

Adam paced back and forth in front of his table as if he were rounding up his own thoughts. "Why did you insist on Lisa having this paternity test in the first place? Did you suspect her of seeing someone else?"

"Yes." Herb let out another uneasy breath.

"And who did you suspect Mr. Louis?"

"My son, Bret." Herb looked directly at Bret when he answered the question.

Bret jumped to his feet and called out, "Objection…"

"Please, sit down Mr. Louis." Judge Knapp ordered. "It's not your place to call objections."

Adam turned back around to face Herb, after having glanced back at Bret's outburst. "Tell the court why you believed your son was also having an affair with Ms. Bixbee."

"I saw him flirting with her and making passes at her on numerous occasions."

Adam thought back to what Eve had said about someone seeing Bret bite Lisa's neck, so he took the chance to see if it was Herb. "Did you ever see him holding her or kissing her?"

"The day she was shot I saw him kissing her on the neck that morning."

Adam's lip curled slightly to one side as he held back the smile that wanted to take full form. Things were pointing more and more towards Bret all the time and his own father was now pointing one of those fingers at him. "Is it possible he was biting her on the neck?"

"It's possible. I do seem to recall her yelling out something when I turned to walk away, but I didn't stick around to find out what was going on."

"That must have been some slap in the face to think she was messing around with your own son right under your nose." Adam pointed out the possible motive Herb might have had. "Did it make you angry in anyway?"

"Not angry enough to kill her if that's where you're headed with this Mr. Webber. I wasn't serious enough about her to care that much. Besides, I knew she'd be leaving the ranch soon enough. If you ask me, I think the girl was out to get her hooks into anyone who had money, whether it was me or Bret."

"And what lengths were you willing to go to see that she didn't get her hooks into either one of you?" Adam raised a brow in question.

"Not murder, Mr. Webber." Herb answered with a stern voice; as if warning Adam to stop pointing fingers before he got bit. "Like I said, I'd already told Lisa she had one month to move on. I felt like that was enough seeing how she was pregnant and it was going to be harder to find work."

"Do you think Bret would have been angry enough to murder if he knew she was seeing you as well as him?"

"Objection your honor that's speculation."

"Overruled." The Judge ordered then nodded toward Herb to go ahead and answer the question.

"I don't know Mr. Webber." Herb gave his honest opinion.

"I have no further questions at this time your honor." Adam walked back around the table to resume his seat.

"Do you have anything further to add Ms. Powers?" The judge turned her attention to the prosecutor.

"No your honor."

"Then you may step down Mr. Louis." Judge Knapp looked down at the paperwork on her desk. "If you have no other witnesses are you ready to give your closing statements?" Diane went on after both attorneys agreed. Then the jury can hopefully deliberate over the weekend so we can wrap this up on Monday."

Before giving her closing statement Powers knew she had lost too much ground to win the case, but she gave it her best effort. After Adam's dynamic closing statement she knew that the jury was in his hands. Even she was convinced of Rachel's innocence, and she had been so sure when the whole trial began that Rachel was the one who shot Lisa Bixbee. But with the new evidence pointing out a man's involvement, it also pointed out the doubt in the minds of the jurors, and the motive of a jealous boyfriend.

Once Adam left the courtroom he stopped in the hallway to check his voice messages. He knew Dixon and Woodrow left early for a reason and he was hoping one of them had called with an explanation. And sure enough there was a message from Dixon, but all he said was that he wanted Adam to come to his office the first chance he got, so Adam walked straight over from the courthouse.

The minute Adam stepped into Dixon's office he began to tell him what the hospital had faxed them. Which wasn't good, since it ruled out both Herb and Bret as the father, leaving them at square one again – without a solid suspect.

"Are you sure this is right?" Adam ran a weary hand through his sun-streaked hair as he questioned the results. "I mean, even Herb seemed to think Bret was the father."

"It's so close to matching with Bret, but only close enough to be a possible family member, but not Herb. In fact, it has less points in common with Herb, than with Bret." Todd interjected. "I used to work the DNA lab before I came to Great Bend, so I've seen enough of these to know what I'm talking about."

"I have no doubt." Adam wasn't about to argue with his knowledge, especially since he had zilch in the forensics field. Rubbing his chin he thought hard about whom it could be, but nothing came to mind. "I'm too tired to even think right now, but I don't know of any other family they have living around here. When his wife left I heard she moved back to Texas, so as far as I know Bailey and Harley are still living there, and Harley would be the only close family I can think of."

"Where in Texas?" Todd was quick to ask. "If Bret has a brother that could be our ticket."

"Now you're pulling straws. What are the chances of Harley having anything to do with this? I just told you how far away he is." Adam scowled.

"It couldn't hurt to at least find out where Harley is living these days and what he's been up to." Dixon wasn't going to rule anything out at this point. There was still a killer out there and he wanted to find him, whoever he was and wherever he was.

Adam threw his hands up in surrender. "Austin was the last I heard. Herb may know better than I would on this."

Chapter 39

Friday evening Adam picked Eve up for dinner around six o'clock. They were celebrating the finalizing of the trial. By Monday or Tuesday the jury should have a verdict, which Adam was pretty confident it would be a not guilty.

Eve enjoyed their time together after not seeing him other than in the courtroom all week. She'd missed talking with him and riding his horses, but she was only willing to verbally admit to missing the riding, at least for now. So it led to them making plans for a Sunday afternoon picnic and horseback ride. The part Eve liked best about the whole plan was that Adam had asked her to bring a change of clothes to church so they could leave from there, which meant he was planning to attend church again.

When they were leaving the restaurant Eve had an uneasy feeling like she was being watched, but she didn't see any dark spirits when she scanned the parking lot. In the setting sun there were a lot of shadows, but that's all she saw – shadows.

Eve stepped off the curb ahead of Adam then looked back to see if he was coming. She waited on him as he held the door for an elderly couple who was also leaving.

Eve could hear a car approaching, but she was still looking at Adam. When Abijah used both hands to force Adam's head to turn in the direction of the oncoming car, Eve's eyes followed as well. A black car with dark tinted windows was coming straight towards her. Adam quickly grabbed Eve's arm and pulled her back up on the curb before she was struck.

The instant the car was in front of them the dark spirit with the tarnished chalice poked his head out through the tinted window and threw an amber colored liquid in Eve's face. She blinked to keep it from getting in her eyes, but when it hit her it was unlike any liquid she's ever known, it was more like a puff of air hitting her. In fact, all she noticed besides a puff of air was a sudden bitter taste in her mouth, even though her mouth hadn't been open either.

Adam felt her tense, but he thought it was from the scare of the car coming so close. "Are you all right?" He asked with concern in his voice. His arms still holding her, not willing to let go just yet.

She was too shook up to respond before the elderly gentleman asked the same question.

"Of course she's not." The elderly man's wife added. "Look at her, she's as pale as a ghost. Do you need to sit down dear?"

Eve managed a thin smile as she raised a hand to decline the offer. "No, thank you. I'll be okay. I just need to get home."

Without a moments hesitation Adam ushered her and her shaky legs over to his jeep. "I only got part of the tag number, did you happen to see any of it?" He was a little shook up too, but he knew he had to be strong for her, so he wasn't about to let it show. He helped her into the jeep before going around to get in himself.

"I closed my eyes, so I'm afraid not." Once in the jeep Eve quickly scanned around to find Hamuel or Abijah. With the top off the jeep she quickly spotted Hamuel above the restaurant battling with Rage. Abijah was coming towards them, so she opened her mouth to ask him, but he was already beginning to answer her.

"*I heard Adam's question and yes, I did see the tag number.*" Abijah answered, then he quoted the numbers to her.

Eve dug a piece of paper out from her purse, wrote down the number and gave it to Adam.

"I thought you had your eyes shut?"

"I did, but Abijah saw the tag so he told me. Did you feel it when he made you turn your head to see that car coming?"

"No. *He* made me turn my head?" Adam gave her a bewildered look when she nodded. "Abijah, that's my angel, right?"

"Yah. Why?"

"I'm just curious as to how many angels it takes to watch over you, that's all." He smiled and pulled his cell phone from his pocket. "I need to call this in before that creep has time to get too far away." Adam called the police station and reported the incident. He knew the make and model of the car, as well as the tag number, thanks to God providing them with guardians. An angel that Adam was now more thankful for, since he had kept Eve from harm. Adam hadn't thought about losing Eve since she'd left the hospital. And he knew her better now than he did then, now he knew her well enough to love her.

After the call to the station Adam took her home and even walked her up to the house and made sure she was okay before he left. He told Peggy what had happened and asked her to keep an eye on Eve, and to call the police if the black Mustang showed up around their house. He informed her that the police were on the lookout for the car, but just in case they weren't in the neighborhood at the time, she needed to call them.

Peggy fully agreed and thanked Adam for all he'd done.

Adam went on home, but he couldn't stop thinking about what happened, and how quickly life could end. He knew now that he was in love with Eve and that it was time to tell her, before it was too late. He also knew that it was time to get things right with God before that was too late as well. It was simply time for change.

He just barely made it home before his emotions caught up with him and engulfed him like a whirlpool. The minute he stepped inside his upstairs apartment he leaned back against the door and slid down to the floor. Cupping his face with his hands he let the emotions flow silently onto his palms.

The loss of Megan and Bradley had left him undone for three years. He wasn't ready to go through it all over again, even if it was on a different scale. After he begged God for forgiveness, he begged him to either take away his feelings for Eve, or to let them have a long life together. He sat there nearly an hour pouring out his heart to God before he pulled himself up to make his way to bed.

Chapter 40

By Sunday morning Keith and his family had heard about the close call Eve had at the restaurant. Which is what prompted Lexi into a decision to get baptized at church that morning. Eve was pleased not only for Lexi, but because it got her parents to attend church that morning with them.

Eve couldn't have been happier. Nearly her whole family was in church, as well as Adam, but mostly because of the new light blazing in Adam's eyes. She couldn't help but notice it the minute he sat down beside her. She also couldn't help but stare at him with an elated grin dancing across her lips.

"Eve." Peggy nudged her daughter with a scowling look. "It's not polite to stare like that."

Eve leaned over and whispered in her mother's ear. "He's finally got the light in his eyes mom." Then she leaned over to her other side where Adam was seated, and whispered to him. "I'm so happy for you."

It took Adam a minute to think about what she meant, then he realized she must have been seeing the light in his eyes. "Oh yah." He pointed towards his face and smiled. "We've got a lot to talk about later."

"I'd say." Eve smiled again.

The service even seemed to lift Eve's spirit, as if she wasn't already lifted high enough. To finish up by seeing Lexi baptized was like the whip topping to finish up a perfect dessert.

What Eve wasn't counting on seeing was all the angels looking in through the roof of the church – illuminating the ceiling with their radiance. Then when Lexi emerged from the water all the angels cheered and sang out, *'Hallelujah. Hallelujah. Her name is written in the Lambs' book of life.'*

The heavenly harmony of all their voices sent a tingle from her head to her toes, and an overwhelming joy filled her heart. Tears swelled up in her eyes and streamed down her smiling face. She had to bite her bottom lip to keep from singing out with the angels as they repeated their song three times.

When Adam noticed her tearful elation he took her hand and held it between both of his.

After the service they all gathered around Keith's car to congratulate Lexi. All of them telling her how happy they were for her decision.

"Now we just need to help your parents get the light back in their eyes." Eve told Lexi as she hugged her.

"Are you going to start that again Eve?" Keith shook his head with unbelief.

"I never ended it Keith." Eve said frankly.

"She does see something very special, so don't take it with a grain of salt." Adam offered his advice.

Keith opened his mouth to say something else until he saw Peggy nodded her head in agreement. Then he didn't know what to say if his own mother was admitting it too.

Eve informed everyone that she was going over to Adam's to ride. Since Keith had driven them to church, Eve grabbed her change of clothes out of his car, and then followed Adam to his jeep.

"I do need to stop by the house to get the coleslaw and dessert I made." Eve told him as he helped her into the jeep.

"Mmmm, did you say dessert?" Adam raised a brow.

Eve nodded her auburn head. "A home made pie, but you'll have to wait to see what flavor."

"If I don't smell it out before then." Adam teased as he climbed up in the driver's seat. Once Eve got back in the jeep after stopping by her house, Adam knew instantly what kind of pie she had in her basket. Taking a deep breath he could easily smell the apples and cinnamon. "No need to say, my nose already knows."

Eve tried to get Adam to tell her about the light in his eyes, but he told her she'd have to wait until they got to eat their dessert. If he had to wait so did she. Eve thought that was fair enough, so she didn't push the issue.

When they reached Eden's ranch Adam went up to his apartment to get the things he'd prepared and to change his clothes. Eve used his bathroom to change clothes. Then he drove them over to the lake under a huge oak tree. Adam spread a tablecloth out over the top of an old weathered picnic table that was sitting in the shade of the tree.

It was turning out to be a perfect September afternoon. The temperature was mild and the light south breeze was non-threatening to their paper plates. With a spectacular view of the lake Eve couldn't help but notice the small rowboat that rested on a meager patch of sand, and the sun dancing out a sparkling invitation across the water.

"Maybe we could go out on the boat instead of riding horses." Eve suggested.

Amusement washed over Adam's face. "Have you been conversing with my angel again?"

"Not today, why?" Eve giggled.

"Because I asked him just this morning if he thought a boat ride would be better than riding horses, since it would be much easier to talk directly facing each other."

"Yes, talk. That's right, you've got a lot to tell me today. Then it's settled. A boat ride it is." Eve gave a finalizing little nod.

Adam made turkey sandwiches on wheat bread with lettuce, tomato, and cheese. He wouldn't tell her what special concoction of salad dressing he made up for his secret bread spread, but it was delicious. He also made up a cucumber salad. Then there was Eve's coleslaw and apple pie, more than enough to fill them beyond need, yet they both saved enough room for a piece of pie.

"I think I'm too stuffed now to climb in the boat." Eve protested.

"I'll help you. Besides, if we wait too long I'm liable to fall asleep from being so full, I need to row a little and work this food down." Adam had too much to tell Eve to let himself fall asleep now, plus he wanted to say it while he still had the nerve.

He helped Eve into the boat, then climbed in behind her after pushing it out into the water. He rowed out around the edge of the lake before stopping on the other side under a spot of shade.

Eve began the conversation by telling Adam about the amber colored liquid that the dark spirit threw at her. After talking with Hamuel she found out the spirits' name was Zarus and that the liquid was bitterness. She explained how this dark spirit carried three different types of liquid in his cup; hatred, bitterness, and greed.

First Adam began by telling Eve how he had given his life back to Christ after returning home Friday evening. Then with a deep breath he went on to tell her, "I also asked him to either take away the feelings I have for you, or to let us have a long life together. Well, come Saturday morning the feelings were still there, so that's when I knew I had to tell you how I'm feeling."

Eve was entranced as she looked across the boat at him. Her heart thundering in her ears as her pulse rushed through her. Hoping and silently praying that his feelings were the same as hers. *'And I didn't think you could give me a more perfect day,'* she silently told God.

Adam swallowed back the lump that was taking form in his throat. "I've fallen in love with you Eve."

'*Thank you Lord.*' Eve's mind silently cried out as tears of joy once again streamed down her cheeks. A smile curled her lips, but no words would come to them.

Adam moved forward onto his knees so that he was directly in front of Eve looking her square in the eye. With both hands he cupped her cheeks and used his thumbs to wipe away the tears. He not only loved the vivid green in her eyes, but the fact that they never concealed a single emotion. "Tell me those are tears of joy and not…"

Eve still found it too hard to speak, so she made a bold move instead, meeting yet another challenge head on - literally. Placing a hand behind his head she pulled his mouth over hers. With all the passion she had locked away, she kissed him like she'd never kissed anyone before, especially since she'd never felt so much love for anyone before.

The world seemed to stand still for a few breathless moments until they finally managed to pull away from each other. Now Adam was the speechless one. She had not only interrupted his sentence, but his train of thought was totally derailed.

"I think I've been in love with you since the first time I heard your voice. Only, like I told you before, I thought you were way too old for me. But every time you'd speak to me when I was blind, my ears would perk up and tingle at the smooth sultry sound of your voice. Even the hairs on the back of my neck would stand at attention to the sound of your voice." With her hand still at the back of his neck Eve let her fingers feel the soft texture of his hair. "I was just never quite sure why, until I got to know you these past few months. I used to think it was because it gave me the creeps to think that a man twice my age would be so persistent about asking me out to lunch," she had to giggle at the shocked look that came over his face. "but now I know it's because my ears loved you even then."

"So do I still give you the creeps and are your ears the only part of you that's in love with me?" He smiled playfully.

"No, now that I've gotten to know you, all of me is in love with all of you." She admitted and pulled him back for another kiss.

Chapter 41

First thing Monday morning Adam was on the phone to Dixon to see if they ever found out whose car it was that nearly ran Eve down.

"It was a rental car." Dixon verified. "Daubs and Woodrow are over at the car lot right now finding out who rented it and to see if they can collect prints or anything. I'll let you know as soon as I hear from them."

"Fair enough." Adam agreed. "And I'll let you know when the jury is done with their deliberations."

"Great. You can reach me on my mobile, since I'm on my way out to Southwind. I've got a few more questions for Herb." Dixon informed him then bid him good-bye. He was out of his chair before he had the phone replaced, and out the door before it had time to ring and stop him again. He wasn't about to wait until the jury was finished deliberating before going on with his investigation. He had to find out who the father of Lisa's child was, and then determine from there if he was the killer or not. But if they didn't come up with some more evidence he wasn't sure they'd ever find the real killer or to be able to prove who the killer was. Yet he just knew there had to be something, and that something had to be somewhere on or near the ranch.

When Dixon pulled up in front of the barn he could hear Herb talking to someone just inside the doorway, so he stepped around to find out who it was. Herb was standing in the office doorway telling Paco to get the manure spreader out of the barn and how he knew he didn't like it being left there.

Paco waved to Dixon as he walked off to go and move the machinery like Herb had asked.

"I recall that sitting there the night Lisa was murdered." Dixon commented.

"Yeah, I remember that too. Especially since I was the one who had to move it and dump it then, because Paco was in jail all weekend, and the crazy thing nearly clogged up on me so I ended up having to dump it into one big pile." Herb let out a frustrated sigh. "So what brings you way out here? I'm sure it's not just to discuss where our spreader is parked."

"No." Dixon chuckled. He was still watching as Paco opened up the other end of the breezeway to back the spreader out. Dixon grew more serious when he noticed the road was just about twenty yards directly out passed that eastside doorway. Someone could have easily slipped out that door without being seen when everyone was gathered around the brood mare pasture. Then Herb's words slowly sank in. "You say it nearly clogged up on you?"

"That's right." Herb frowned with misunderstanding. "What difference does that make?"

"It could mean a lot." Dixon walked down to where the spreader was just as Paco started it up. "Wait a second." He called up to Paco and he shut off the tractor. Dixon examined the back of the spreader where the blades were. His eyes looked over every blade until he found it. Then he pulled out the notebook from his pocket and collected the tiny white fiber in the fold of a piece of paper he tore from the notebook. "Can you show me where you dumped it at?"

"Sure, if you're really interested in seeing a big pile of manure." Herb laughed. "We'll drive my truck out there."

Dixon followed him to his truck and got in the passenger seat. Herb drove them out the south drive that went between the mare and gelding pens, then down alongside the river to an open field past the gelding's pen. Sure enough it was the biggest pile Dixon had ever seen. Herb had backed the spreader up to a drop off next to the riverbank where he could dump the whole load into one pile. Something told him the missing evidence was there.

Dixon pulled out his cell phone and called for a team to be sent out and scan the area. To make sure there was nothing tampered with, Dixon had to wait there in the sun until the team arrived, which took them about an hour to get there. It gave him plenty of time to scan the area for footprints, which he did find one faint print in the soft dirt at the edge of the river. It was from a boot, but there was no way of knowing whose boot or if it was significant to the case, until a match was ran on it.

The wait was well worth it when the team uncovered the missing evidence. They found the missing pillow, with a few things stuffed inside it, like a bloodstained bandanna wrapped around the missing bullet casing. There was also a white T-shirt with blood spatters found in the manure pile. It was all bagged and tagged and rushed to the lab without delay.

"I know you didn't just come all the way out here to look through my manure, so why did you come out here Dixon?" Herb asked as they drove back up to the barn.

"Oh, yah. I came out here to tell you that Bret wasn't the father of Lisa's baby either. So you were either wrong about them, or she was playing someone else as well. I was hoping you might have a second idea as to who that might have been."

"She didn't do a lot away from the ranch. She was either on the road with me helping at cutting events, or she was here, so I have no other ideas."

"Well, I'll have to hope this missing evidence turns up something then." Dixon let out a heavy breath. "Let me know if you think of anyone, will ya?"

"Sure." Herb complied easily.

Dixon was about to leave when his phone rang. It was Daubs calling to tell him that the car was rented under Herb's name, but that the prints collected matched with Bret's. So Dixon took Bret back to the station with him for questioning.

At first Bret tried to deny it, but the evidence wouldn't let him, so Bret finally fessed up. "I wasn't trying to kill her, only to make her stop poking her nose into my family and stirring up trouble. We're innocent, but she's trying to make us look guilty."

"You do enough of that on your own, so I can see why you wouldn't want anyone helping you."

Dixon added his opinion, then sent Bret down to be booked.

Herb bailed Bret out, so he wasn't in jail more than an hour before getting to go back home. Which frustrated Dixon to no end, but there was nothing he could do about it.

Chapter 42

Tuesday afternoon Lolita served lunch to Herb and Bret then went back into the kitchen to start cleaning up. Lolita tried hard not to ease drop, but the sound of their voices carried all too well, especially when they grew louder with every word. It was the first time she'd heard them speak, since Herb had bailed Bret out on Monday.

Herb was grumbling to Bret about his foolish choice; to rent the car and play tag with Eve. From his tone it was obvious that he was very unhappy with Bret. "It's crazy stunts like this that make me question if you're really my son. Maybe the hospital got the paternity tests mixed up and Harley was the real son instead of you."

Bret's face reddened as Rage sank his talons deeper into his mind and filled his head with thoughts that burst forth like molten lava. "Yeah, you would've liked that better, since he was always your favorite, right up until you found out he wasn't even yours. It took me a few months, but I figured out that's why you made 'em both leave once Harley was well enough to travel." He bellowed out.

"You bet your boots I made 'em leave. Bailey had me believing Harley was my son all those years, so once I found out he wasn't I couldn't stand the sight of either one of 'em." Herb bellowed back in an equally heated tone. "That's why I wasn't about to let Lisa pull the same game with me."

Lolita covered her mouth to muffle the heavy breath that rushed into her lungs. She never knew that was why they had divorced. She thought it was because Bailey was tired of Herb's obsessive behavior. But now it made sense as to why Harley was the only one who left with her, and why she even severed all ties with Bret.

Herb pushed his plate away, since he'd lost his appetite. "I'm just glad I listened to my father and made Bailey sign a prenuptial agreement, or she would've had everything she was out to take me for. And if you want to stay in my will you'd better start listening to me more and stop running around acting like a mad man."

"Maybe I am a mad man." Bret sneered, exactly as Rage did in the unseen world. "Besides, you don't have anyone else to leave your precious fortune to anyway, so how can you take me out of your will?"

"Don't you worry, I can think of any number of charity's who would love to have a large donation."

Bret's eyes widened. "You wouldn't?"

"Don't push me to find out." Herb said flatly through narrowed eyes. "As far as Eve Kincaid, you stay away from her and no more of this foolishness. And never, ever, use my name again like you did when you rented that car." He got up and walked away from the table.

Lolita took shallow breaths until her heart settled down from the tense conversation. She hadn't wanted to hear any of it, but now that she did, she wasn't sure she should keep it to herself. She was in question as to whether or not Herb was the one who had killed Lisa for trying to pull the same game Bailey had. But at the same time, if she told anyone she'd lose her job, since he was her boss. Once she finished the dishes she talked to Paco about it and asked him what she should do.

"Don't be loca muchacha." Paco told his sister. "If we lose our jobs we lose our home. We can't say we think señor Louis killed someone without proof, and even if we did have proof, then where would we live and work once he was arrested?"

Lolita didn't know the answer, so she just shrugged and agreed to keep things to herself. Although she didn't like it, she just didn't know what else to do about it. She didn't want to find a new job and a new home all at the same time, especially since a job itself was hard enough to come by at the present time. And neither one of them had any other job skills except for the work they'd done for Herb over the past ten years.

At one o'clock the jury was done with lunch and with the deliberation. They came back into the courtroom with a verdict.

Eve patted Rachel on the shoulder as she took a seat directly behind her and Adam. "It'll be fine." She softly reassured the girl.

"Thanks." Rachel pursed her lips into a thin smile. Her eyes met with her mothers' as she offered a reassuring smile to her. Rachel's boyfriend was there to offer his support too, even though it was a risk to his job, because of all the time he already took off to be in court with her. What surprised her was seeing Herb there, since she wasn't sure if he was there for support, or just to hear the verdict. But she was willing to give him the benefit of the doubt and chalked him off as a concerned employer.

Eve could sense the tension rise as the judge asked the jury for their verdict. Then one of the members handed off their written verdict to the bailiff, who then handed it off to the judge.

Diane Knapp read the verdict, first to herself, then to the court. "This court finds the defendant, Rachel Ann Meade, on the charge of first degree murder, not guilty."

Eve saw the peace that washed over Rachel as she let her shoulders relax. She also heard the angels outside let out a little cheer for Rachel.

Knapp continued down the list of charges. "This court finds the defendant, Rachel Ann Meade, on the charge of second degree murder, not guilty. However, this court finds the defendant, Rachel Ann Meade, on the charge of mishandling a firearm, guilty. She will pay a fee of two hundred dollars, she will be required to take a hunter's safety course and do thirty days of community service."

"That's something I can handle way better than jail time." Rachel leaned over to tell Adam. "Thank you so much for all you've done."

"You're quite welcome. But give your thanks to God." Adam offered a smile as he closed his briefcase and stood up. "I'll let you know when and where you'll begin the community service."

Eve was glad everything had all worked out. But she was troubled to think there was still a killer on the loose out there somewhere. She had been praying hard for God to show her who the killer was, but so far she'd gotten nothing, not even another hunch about where to look.

"Are you still coming out to ride this evening?" Adam asked Eve as they left the courtroom together. After she nodded he went on to inform her. "I need to stop by the store on the way home then, because I'd like you to come out for dinner as well."

Eve agreed and used his cell phone to call and let her mother know where she'd be. Eve waited for Adam in his jeep at the super market and she saw Paco and Lolita coming out of the store. They walked right by the jeep, so Eve said hello to both of them.

After they both greeted Eve back, Lolita asked Paco a few questions in Spanish, and Paco returned his answer in Spanish.

Although Eve understood every word they said, she didn't acknowledge it. "What did she ask you?" Eve probed to see if Lolita would offer anymore helpful information.

"Ah…" Paco hesitated, then lied. "She was just asking me where we know you from."

Unseen

Lolita rattled off a few more things in Spanish before Paco apologized to Eve and then ushered his sister on to their truck before she said too much. Eve understood his concern to their jobs, but she wished he would've let Lolita say more. Paco's sister definitely knew more than he was letting her say, it made Eve wonder if she didn't know who the killer was, and from Paco's concern about their jobs it had to be one of the Louis'.

Chapter 43

First thing Wednesday morning Eve went to Dixon's office explaining what she overheard. Eve told him word for word what Lolita and Paco had said, "She asked Paco if they should tell me about Herb, how he wasn't about to let Lisa pull the same game as Bailey. And about the test he had done to find out that Harley wasn't his son. But Paco didn't want her to say anything, because of their jobs at the ranch, so he told her to go get in the truck. That's when she said that they had to do something if Herb was the killer. Paco told her to stop talking crazy and get in the truck before he left without her. Then he made her go with him to the truck, after lying to me about what they were saying."

Dixon got up and walked over to look out his window. "It's all just hearsay. He said she said. All I can really do with this is ask a few questions and check into hospital records and hope that this paternity test went through the hospital here in Dodge. Otherwise this could be just another dead end. I'm still waiting to hear back from Todd on the evidence that we just sent to the lab, but it'll be at least Friday before we know anything on the DNA from the T-shirt."

"Chief Crow's daughter works at the hospital in medical records, so she should be able to help you get those together." Eve reminded him.

"I'm counting on it, but whatever they do have on Bailey Louis will be at least ten years old, paternity tests have come along way since then." Dixon reflected, pacing back and forth between his chair and the window. "Just when I think I've got this figured out, I run into a dead end. Bret or Herb either one could have done this, even though we know neither of them fathered Lisa's child. Jealousy is enough motive for either one of those hot heads. Bret sure is acting very suspicious, yet Herb's got the most to lose. If I find anything relevant I'll fax it to Todd and have him do a comparison." He thanked Eve for the information and walked her out of the building.

While Eve was waiting at the corner to cross the street, she saw the same black Mustang coming through the intersection. She held her breath and thought that surely Bret wouldn't pull the same stunt again, but just in case she stepped back a safe distance from the curb.

The car past by at a normal speed this time, but once again the same dark spirit popped his head out through the dark tinted window and tossed more of his bitter liquid on her. Hamuel was quick enough to block most of the liquid from splashing in her face, but some of it hit her chest. This time it was a black liquid, which was hatred according to Hamuel. She didn't get a bitter taste in her mouth; instead she felt a twinge of pain shoot through her heart. She also didn't see the tag number once again.

"Please follow that car Hamuel and find out where this spirit is coming from and why he keeps attacking me."

Without hesitation Hamuel was gone. No doubt following the car as she had asked. She shuddered at first to think that it meant she was left unprotected, but she said a silent prayer that it wouldn't take him long. Once she finally made it across the street, she told Adam about the car just before she entered the courtroom to transcribe a hearing.

Since Adam didn't have to appear in court until later, he got on his cell phone to Dixon and reported the car once more. He couldn't imagine even Bret being foolish enough to rent that car again and pull another stunt. Dixon assured him he'd look into that while he was looking into everything else.

Dixon and Daubs spent hours at the hospital looking through boxes for the old records on Bailey. The hospital didn't keep records filed on computers ten years ago, so they had to go about finding them through the long process. But they did manage to find what they were looking for, which was a grateful surprise to Dixon. Which made him all the more suspicious of Herb. After having one woman lie to him about a child being his, it would be intolerable for another woman to do the very same thing, possibly even to the point of murder.

"Maybe now we need to look up this ex-wife of Herb's and see what her side of this story was like." Dixon held up the file towards Colby.

"I heard she moved to Austin, Texas when she left here."

Colby confirmed what Dixon had also heard, so Dixon nodded in agreement. "It may mean a trip to Texas for us, are you up for that?"

"Did you say something about a road trip?" Colby pulled the keys from his pocket with a young mischievous grin.

"Let's fax this to Todd and make a few calls." After saying that, Dixon headed for the door, and his long strides made a quick exit from the hospital.

Through the phone calls Dixon made, he found out that Bailey had died in a car accident just six short months after leaving Dodge. From what the Austin police said, Harley had made a big stink saying that Herb was at fault, but there was never any proof of that to even make an arrest. As far as everything appeared, it was simply an accident and Bailey had simply run her car off the road.

With that information Dixon was anxious to talk to Harley and find out why he thought Herb was guilty. He found out Harley had worked as a live-in wrangler on several different ranches after his mother's death, but Harley's trail vanished a year ago. The last rancher Harley worked for said that all he knew was that Harley was running with the rodeo circuit and staying somewhere in Kansas.

After spending the rest of his shift on the phone Dixon felt like he'd ran into yet another dead end. For all he knew at this point Harley could be dead too. He hadn't even been able to locate any of Bailey's family, except her deceased parents. Plus the black Mustang hadn't even been rented from the same rental agency; in fact, none of the local rental agencies had rented out a black Mustang. So the car appeared to have vanished too.

That night when Eve was out in the back yard with her dog, she noticed Abijah was sitting on her roof instead of Hamuel, so she called him down to find out what was going on.

"As Adam drove home he requested in his prayer that I watch over you until Hamuel returned." Abijah explained to her.

It warmed her heart to think that Adam would leave himself unprotected to make sure she had protection. She had told him how she sent Hamuel after the car to find out where it went, which is how he knew she was unprotected in the first place. So she said a special blessing over him in her prayers that night, as well as a special prayer for Hamuel, since he still hadn't returned by the time she went to bed. She didn't know what could be taking him so long to follow a car, unless he was battling with a lot of dark spirits wherever his pursuit had led him.

Chapter 44

Hamuel returned sometime in the night, only Eve didn't talk to him until she woke up Thursday morning. Then she found out how far he tracked the car and where it went, which was nearly to Wichita. Hamuel told her that the car stopped in Kingman, Kansas. There the woman got out and went into a house. She came out with a man and they got into a truck, drove to an arena, spent a few hours there before returning to the house and going to bed. Since they were the only ones in the house it appeared to be their home.

Hamuel didn't know who the man was, and he guessed that the spirit had attacked Eve, simply because he knew she could see him. But the woman he had seen in the courtroom talking with Tracy Powers, Lisa Bixbee's twin sister, Felicia.

Eve was stunned by Hamuel's report. "What connection is this to the crime? Or is it any connection at all?" Eve asked out loud more to herself than to Hamuel. "But this Zarus was in the courtroom pouring out his hatred on Bret when he was on the stand. Was that just because Lisa's twin hates Bret because of the loss of her sister? Plus the fact that Bret rented a car identical to Felicia's car, that's an odd coincidence. There's got to be some type of connection here."

"*Possibly.*" Hamuel agreed. "*There are many ways things can be connected.*"

Peggy stepped out onto the back porch to see whom Eve was talking to. "It's awful early in the morning to be talking to yourself." She offered a thin smile before taking a sip of her coffee.

"That's why I talk to angels." Eve smiled back.

Peggy pointed to the empty chair next to Eve. "I won't be sitting on your angels' lap if I sit there will I?"

"No." Eve giggled. "He's actually sitting on the edge of the roof right there." She pointed to the small overhang over the back door.

"You're up extra early for work this morning. Are you that glad to be back at work?"

"I guess." Eve responded with a nod. "But mostly I'm concerned over the fact that there's still a killer running around out there somewhere. I thought I knew who it was, but even I'm not that sure anymore."

"The devil is the master of confusion, so try praying about it, the Lord will show you in good time." Peggy advised.

Eve had been doing just that, but it obviously wasn't time yet, because she didn't know who it was.

The rest of the day Eve rolled things over in her mind. It was hard concentrating on her job because of her preoccupied thoughts. She didn't' get to see Adam until after work, since he wasn't scheduled to be in court again until Monday. But once she did see him she told him what Hamuel had found out for her.

"If we share this information with the detective, we're going to have to tell him about your ability to see into the spiritual realm, and how do you think that will go over?" Adam questioned to her over his desk.

Eve shrugged her shoulders. "I do see the light in his wife's eyes, but not his, so I imagine he knows about such things. Do you think it'd be better if we told him with his wife present so she could help him understand?"

"I guess that depends on how many people you want to know about this. You used to want to keep it to yourself, since you had run into doubt among your own family." Adam reminded her. "Besides, you don't know how, or even if, this is in anyway related to Lisa's murder."

With that in mind, she decided not to involve Katrina. But she did want to tell Dixon about it the first chance she had, which wouldn't be until Friday, since he was probably already home for the day. She didn't want to bother him with this at home like they had concerning the stationary paper. That had been solid evidence, this was more hearsay, as Dixon would approach it. But she felt he needed to know, if for no other reason, to let him know where the second black Mustang disappeared.

"Dixon is suppose to call me on Friday as soon as he gets back the results on the tests, so I'll call you right after he calls me. Then we can go tell him your news together, if you'd like." Adam said as he cleared off his desk by stuffing the files into his briefcase. "I've got a dinner meeting with a client this evening, but you're welcome to joins us if you'd like."

"I can't this evening. We're suppose to go over and have dinner with Keith and Lou Ann." A bright smile parted Eve's lips. "But I made sure I kept Friday night open."

Adam smiled in return. "That's good, because I made plans for us." As much as Adam hated leaving her with a quick simple kiss, he was in too big of a hurry to do more than just that. But he'd make up for it on Friday, when he let her in on his big plans for their evening.

Eve didn't think life could get any better when she saw the light in Keith and Lou Ann's eyes at dinner that night. It was so exciting that she commented on it the moment she saw them. That was also the moment Keith became a believer in Eve's miracle, especially since neither of them had said anything about it to Peggy or Eve, so there was no other way she could've known other than to actually see the light for herself.

Chapter 45

Woodrow called Dixon with the results on the T-shirt just before lunch. He informed Dixon that the blood on the T-shirt was a positive match with Lisa's blood, but that the other DNA collected from the shirt didn't match with anyone from Southwind, although it was a match with the fetus.

"So whoever was wearing the shirt is no doubt the father to Lisa's child." Dixon concluded into his end of the phone. "What did you come up with on the paternity tests I faxed you from the hospital?"

"It looks like the father of Lisa's child is none other than Harley James Louis."

"Wow, now this case is really taking a turn. How'd he end up in the picture? According to Herb he hasn't even seen Harley since him and Bailey left ten years ago. And if Lisa didn't leave the ranch much without Herb, where'd she find the time to see Harley? This means Harley must be living close by." Dixon let out a heavy sigh. "His trail stopped somewhere in Kansas, but I have no idea where. I guess I'll have to try harder now to find out where."

"Looks that way. We also collected a partial bloody print from the bullet casing, but we haven't got a match on that yet." Todd confirmed. "Have you tried searching for him under his mother's maiden name?"

"No, I haven't, thanks, that's a great idea." Dixon hung up the phone and called Colby into his office to ask him to run a computer search on a Harley James Louis or a Harley James Windsor. Then he got on the phone himself to make a few calls, Adam being one of those calls. It kept Dixon so busy he didn't even take time to stop for lunch. And it kept him after work waiting on Adam and Eve to come by to talk to him.

Dixon didn't know what to say after Eve had finished telling him about the ordeal with the second black Mustang and how she could see into the spiritual world. He wasn't even sure he could argue the issue with her, since he knew he'd grown cold towards the Lord, and that he probably didn't have any light in his eyes. But he knew his wife was still strong for the Lord, as Eve had put it, and that she was sure to still have the light within her.

"I don't know if this is even relevant to my case or not, but I'll look into it." That was all Dixon could manage to say. He'd never known people in modern times to have such revelations happen in their lives, but he did believe it was possible.

"I don't know either." Eve admitted. "But something keeps telling me there's a connection somehow. Just like that *something* that kept telling me to go to Southwind the day I got the stationary page."

Dixon couldn't deny that she had been onto something then, so perhaps she was onto something now. Although he couldn't for the life of him figure out what Lisa's sister would have to do with her death, if anything. Unless revenge or sibling rivalry was the motive, or a possible life insurance policy. If it did indeed have a connection, but it could very well be completely coincidental. It was going to be tricky to even investigate, since there was no justifiable reason for a search warrant. He'd have to come up with a reason to even speak to the girl, which was going to take some thought.

For his big plans, Adam took Eve out for dinner and a movie that evening, which was the first time Eve had ever gone to a theater to see a movie. She'd never been able to see them before July, so she'd never gone. It was a sappy romance movie too, which was somewhat of a surprise to Eve that Adam would pick a movie like that. She figured he'd like the action type movies better, and possibly he was simply thinking of what she'd like to watch over himself. In any case, Eve had a delightful evening with him as usual, more so now that they were holding hands or arm in arm. She found it very cozy to snuggle up beside him in the theater.

What Eve wasn't expecting was the question Adam was about to ask her. He stopped her at the back door and had her sit down in one of the lawn chairs on the patio. Then he kneeled down on one knee in front of her just like the guy in the movie had done. "Evelyn Kincaid," He started as he pulled a royal blue velvet box out of his pocket. "Will you love me for the rest of my life and accept me as your husband?" He opened the box to reveal the solitary diamond ring.

Eve was speechless as the lump in her throat swelled and tears rolled from her eyes. She hadn't expected him to ask this question so soon, although she had hoped he would eventually ask. All she could manage to do was nod her head so that he'd know she heard and accepted his offer of marriage.

A bright smile creased his tanned cheeks. "I know I'm moving pretty fast for you, but I've been alone for three years now, so I don't want to waste anymore time, but I'll let you decide how long of an engagement we should have. I was thinking about Valentine's Day, which will give you five months to plan things out. What do you think about that?"

Eve was still speechless, so she did the next best thing; she pulled him to her for a kiss. She thought she'd be able to think over the date while kissing him, but all she could think about was being able to kiss him for the rest of her life, a thought that filled her with complete joy.

Once Eve could swallow back the lump and dry her eyes, she managed to find her voice again. "That sounds very romantic, but I'm not sure I want to wait five months. If you want to get married on a holiday, Thanksgiving is just a few months away, and that would give me even more to be thankful for this year."

The smile on Adam's face deepened. "Sounds wonderful to me, and here I was worried that you'd think I was moving too fast."

"I can already see the colors I'd choose for my wedding too. Orange and beige. Aren't those Fall colors?"

Adam nodded before kissing her again. Until an idea hit him, then he pulled away to voice it out. "Instead of having the flower girl throw flowers, we could have her toss bright fall colored leaves down the isle. Do you think Lexi would like to do that?"

Then he slid the ring on her finger and smiled when it was a perfect fit.

"Sounds like we're working up a plan." Eve giggled and stared down at the ring on her finger. Even under the dim yellow porch light it gleamed like a star in the night. Then she silently thanked God for the perfect ending to the perfect week, and for blessing her with the perfect man.

She made Adam go inside with her to tell her mother the good news. Of course Peggy thought they were moving too fast, but she had come to like Adam and knew that he'd make her daughter a good husband, so she didn't want to get in the way of their happiness. Although she did try to suggest they give her more time to help plan her only daughter's wedding, but her attempt was like blowing smoke into the wind.

Chapter 46

First thing Monday morning Dixon was on the phone to Herb asking him a few more questions regarding Harley. He found out that the reason Herb had the paternity test ran in the first place, was because Harley had lost a lot of blood when he was gored by a bull and needed a blood transfusion. When neither Herb nor Bailey could be blood donors for their own son, he began checking into why. They nearly lost Harley, because they had to wait for blood to be transferred in, since his blood type was rare and the hospital didn't have enough on hand at the time.

Herb was shocked when Dixon told him that Harley was the father of Lisa's unborn child. "I can't believe he was here...on my ranch...and I didn't even know it. Are you sure about all of this?"

"The evidence don't lie." Dixon confirmed. "What would Harley stand to gain? Do you think he was trying to frame you or Bret?"

"I don't know... possibly. He could have a number of motives. I'm sure he's still mad about being cut out of my will and cut off from my money. Plus he thinks I'm responsible for Bailey's death somehow."

"Were you even in Austin, Texas at the time of Bailey's accident?"

"I was at a cutting event, but I never saw her, and I didn't even go out with the guys that night after the event. I knew she was in town somewhere and I didn't want to risk running into her, so I went back to my hotel room with a lady friend." Herb admitted. "If you find him, let me know, will ya?"

Dixon agreed before hanging up the phone. Now he was beginning to see Harley's motives, and how he could easily have more than one as Herb had put it. Now the big question was how to find him. So far they hadn't come up with anything on the computer search under either name. Which all that meant was that Harley was probably working at another ranch where they were paying him cash under the table.

Dixon looked into the lead on the other black Mustang that Eve had told him about. When he ran a check on Felicia Bixbee, he got a Wichita address, not one in Kingman. So he was afraid it would turn up as another dead end, but he drove to Kingman with Colby anyway, just to be a man of his word. He also thought it'd be good for both of them to get out of the office for a little road trip.

There was no answer at the address Eve had given them in Kingman. There was also no black Mustang or even a truck in the driveway. They were about to get back in their car to leave when Colby noticed the elderly woman next door out in her flower garden.

"Let's see if she knows who lives here." Colby suggested nodding his head towards the lady's house.

Dixon took the lead and approached the woman. "Excuse me ma'am, do you know who lives next door to you?"

"I sure do young man. I've still got all my wits about me ya know." She glared at them through aged squinted eyes.

"As I'm sure you do ma'am. Can you tell me her name?"

"Well, it ain't no her, that's for sure." The lady laughed, showing off her rotting teeth, then she brushed her hands together to dust them off. "He's a very manly man, if ya know what I mean, a cowboy who'd just assume stomp ya for referrin' to him as a her." She laughed again. "His name's Louis or Harley, somethin' like that. He works for Ramsey's farm just off of 54. You can either find him there, or he'll be at the rodeo arena this weekend for sure, just like clockwork."

"Thank you very much ma'am, you've been very helpful." Dixon offered a smile then he gave Colby a sideward glance that stated they were both thinking the same thing. Dixon couldn't believe they actually stumbled upon the very thing they were looking for. Eve had been right in directing them there, even if it was for an entirely different reason.

Once they got directions to the ranch they were back out on the road. When they reached the ranch they saw a group of guys standing around the corral fence watching another man riding a bucking horse inside the pen. They were all cheering and going on until Dixon and Colby pulled up beside them.

Even though Colby wasn't in uniform, Dixon still had on one of his usual suits, so it was a dead give away that they were somehow affiliated with the law.

The gray haired man at the fence, and apparently the owner, walked over to meet them as they got out of their car. "Can I help you folks?"

"Yes, we're looking for Harley Louis." Dixon spoke out.

"Well, then you'd be looking for that man right out there on top that horse." He motioned behind him to the corral. "Why are you lookin' for him?"

"We're with the Dodge City police department and we've found evidence that puts him at a crime scene, so we'll need to take him back with us for some questioning." Dixon explained and showed his badge.

The man looked completely shocked by the news. "Harley's such a nice kid. I don't see how he could've done anything wrong. He may have a quick temper, but there's no law against that." The man's mouth was still open with shock as he followed the two policemen back to the corral.

Dixon and Colby waited for Harley to finish with the horse and dismount. Harley didn't deny who he was, but he did clam not to know what they were talking about.

Harley stated that he had been at a rodeo the weekend in question. "That's what I do every weekend." He had stated. "You can ask anyone who knows me. They'll tell you I live to rodeo."

Harley called out to his employer to get him a lawyer as Dixon and Colby were toting him back to their car.

Driving back with the prime suspect in tow Dixon felt like he'd finally put in a good day's work. Now he just prayed that the evidence on Harley was enough to convict him and put him away where he belonged. He still wasn't sure how the black Mustang and Felicia Bixbee fit into all of this, but he was hopeful about that truth prevailing as well.

Chapter 47

Dixon was unable to get anything out of Harley. He kept claiming that he was at a rodeo during the time of Lisa's death, even though his DNA evidence placed him at the scene that night. When they checked out Harley's story they found out that his name was on the rodeo docket, but that it had been scratched because he was a no show. He even tried to deny knowing Felicia, until she showed up at the end of the week to bail him out. Which is how Dixon found out where she fit into the whole picture.

Dixon took Felicia aside to ask her a few questions. She didn't have enough money to bail Harley out, and he was sure she wouldn't even want to once she realized what he was in there for. "Do you know why he's even in jail?"

"Not really. Kyle Ramsey said that he was accused of being at a crime scene or something. But you've got the wrong man, he's only in Dodge City two weeks a year for the big rodeo." Felicia insisted.

"Our evidence says otherwise. We found a T-shirt with his sweat and your sister's blood on it." Dixon's voice softened when he saw the shock on Felicia's face. "That tells us that he was here the night she was shot."

"That doesn't mean he did it." She still insisted through the mist of tears swelling in her eyes.

Dixon dropped his head into a frustrated hand and carefully thought over his words. Looking back up at her, his eyes filled with compassion as he spoke. "Your sister was pregnant with his child. We think that was part of the reason he killed her."

Felicia's eyes filled with tears and all she could say was "No." It was too much for her to believe, too much for her to want to believe. After a long hard cry, she finally managed to say more than 'no.' "Are you one hundred percent sure about this?"

"Yes, I'm afraid so." Dixon assured her.

Felicia shook her head. "Then why would he kill her? Why would he string both of us along like this?"

"You'll have to ask him that yourself, we can't seem to get any answers at all out of him." Dixon verified with a heavy sigh. "How and where did you met Harley?"

"There was this rodeo in Wichita a year ago that a couple of my friends took me to. Come to think of it, he thought I was Lisa, that's why he came over to talk to me. Once I managed to convince him I was her identical twin, he said he'd met Lisa at a cutting event in Texas. We got to talking, since he knew more about Lisa then I did at that time. I hadn't talked to Lisa for a whole year. I had totally lost track of her. She moved around so much it was hard keeping up with her over two and a half years." Felicia recalled.

Dixon talked Felicia into seeing if she could get some answers out of Harley and she willingly agreed. He knew it was going to be hard on her, since she was obviously in love with the guy.

Felicia wasn't sure what to ask first, so she started with the least painful question first. "Were you seeing me and Lisa both at the same time?" After his curt nod she blinked back the threat of tears, telling herself to cowgirl-up and swallow down the bitterness that flooded her heart. "So, did you get her pregnant then?"

"Is that what they told you?" Harley asked and reached for her hands to comfort her, only to have her withdraw them from the tabletop as she nodded. "It wasn't suppose to work like that." He finally admitted. "She was suppose to get pregnant with Herb's baby, not mine, she ruined the whole plan."

"The whole plan?" Felicia's eyes narrowed. "What plan?"

"She was supposed to have Herb's child so I could get my share of the inheritance through the baby, but she messed it all up. I knew he'd never buy it a second time around."

"Buy what?"

Harley frowned at her like she should know what he was talking about. "The baby bit. I knew he'd have a test done right away and sure enough, he did, he didn't even wait until they were home from the cutting event."

Felicia could no longer hide the hurt. "Then you did kill her…because she messed up your plans."

Zarus was having a field day in the unseen world. His tarnished cup was sloshing liquid in all directions. Splashing black all over Felicia, then green and amber liquid all over Harley, laughing the entire time. Back and forth he hurled his cup.

"I didn't need her anymore, I had you and a new plan, only I heard someone coming before I had a chance to get her body out of there."

Felicia's eyes widened in horror. "A new plan. What new plan? Whose body, Lisa's?"

"I was going to send you there as if nothing had ever happened to Lisa and..."

"You're a total mad man." Felicia jumped to her feet. "Do you think for one second that I'd be your next pawn in this sick twisted little game of yours? Were you going to send me there to bear Herb's child just so you could get to his money?"

Zarus laughed with glee as he poured all three of his toxic potions over Harley's head, green, amber and black, all spilling out from his cup at once.

A deep crease hardened Harley's brow. "Part of that should have been mine. For nineteen years he treated me like a son, he loved me like a son, and then he just threw us out to the dogs. As if that wasn't enough, six months later he killed my mother, he took everything away from me."

"Boy, I never thought she'd get him to talk this much. He must not realize this is a two-way glass." Dixon commented to Colby as they listened from the other side of the glass.

"Either that or he is a mad man." Colby shook his head.

"Let's hope not, we want him to go to jail, not a mental institute." Dixon huffed.

"Did you ever thank Eve for sending us to Kingman?"

A wide grin crossed Dixon's face. "Yes, I did. And you know what?"

"What?"

"Her and Adam are getting married in November. In fact, Adam asked me to be his best man."

"Boy that was quick." Colby shook his head with amazement.

"Quick! Actually, I'm surprised Adam took this long. I saw the way he looked at that girl the first time he saw her walk into the courtroom. If she could have seen it, she wouldn't have kept turning down his offers for lunch." Dixon let out a soft laugh.

"Do you think we've got enough on tape now to stop it?" Colby smiled and walked towards the recorder.

"I'd say we got just enough rope to hang him. Go ahead and shut it off before he does start showing signs of a mad man. That just goes to show how vicious greed can be. Here's a man more interested in getting his share of money and revenge, than he is in love. And here he not only had one, but two, beautiful women willing to do almost anything for him." Dixon exited the room to save Felicia from hearing anymore. He knew it had to be hard on her to find out that the man she loved not only didn't love her in return, but he was seeing her sister before killing her.

The whole thing made Dixon realized he needed to get back in church before the evil in the world consumed him. Word around the station was that Darwin Talbot, now serving his seventy-year sentence for vehicular manslaughter, was witnessing to everyone in prison. For Darwin to wake up and turn back to the Lord it had cost the life of an innocent girl. Much like the higher price that was paid at Calvary, when Christ willingly offered his own life, so that man could find forgiveness of sin.

To order additional copies of

UNSEEN

Have your credit card ready and call:

1-877-421-READ (7323)

or please visit our web site at
www.pleasantword.com

Also available at:
www.amazon.com
and
www.barnesandnoble.com

Printed in the United States
38980LVS00001B/7-18